# "I Haven't Saved Myself All These Years To Toss Away My Virginity To The First Man Who Shows Me A Little Attention!"

The moment the words were out, Penny clapped a hand over her mouth, her face draining of color. With a strangled sob she ran for her room.

Erik winced at the furious slam of the door.

*A virgin? Had his mousy secretary just confessed to being a virgin?*

He shook his head. No way, he told himself. She couldn't be a virgin. Not with a body like that.

At the thought, an image pushed itself into his mind of her standing in the ballroom in that dress. The clingy, glittery fabric hugged her body like a second skin, accentuating a slender waist and full sensuous hips.

He groaned, knowing he'd never get to sleep that night. Not when he knew a virgin slept in the room across from his....

Dear Reader,

Welcome to the world of Silhouette Desire, where you can indulge yourself every month with romances that can only be described as passionate, powerful and provocative!

The always fabulous Elizabeth Bevarly offers you May's MAN OF THE MONTH, so get ready for *The Temptation of Rory Monahan.* Enjoy reading about a gorgeous professor who falls for a librarian busy reading up on how to catch a man!

The tantalizing Desire miniseries TEXAS CATTLEMAN'S CLUB: LONE STAR JEWELS concludes with *Tycoon Warrior* by Sheri WhiteFeather. A Native American ex-military man reunites with his estranged wife on a secret mission that renews their love.

Popular Peggy Moreland returns to Desire with a romance about a plain-Jane secretary who is in love with her *Millionaire Boss.* The hero-focused miniseries BACHELOR BATTALION by Maureen Child continues with *Prince Charming in Dress Blues,* who's snowbound in a cabin with an unmarried woman about to give birth! *Baby at His Door* by Katherine Garbera features a small-town sheriff, a beautiful stranger and the bundle of love who unites them. And Sara Orwig writes a lovely tale about a couple entering a marriage of convenience in *Cowboy's Secret Child.*

This month, Silhouette is proud to announce we've joined the national campaign "Get Caught Reading" in order to promote reading in the United States. So set a good example, and get caught reading all six of these exhilarating Desire titles!

Enjoy!

*Joan Marlow Golan*

Joan Marlow Golan
Senior Editor, Silhouette Desire

Please address questions and book requests to:
Silhouette Reader Service
U.S.: 3010 Walden Ave., P.O. Box 1325, Buffalo, NY 14269
Canadian: P.O. Box 609, Fort Erie, Ont. L2A 5X3

# Millionaire Boss
## PEGGY MORELAND

Silhouette® Desire®

Published by Silhouette Books
America's Publisher of Contemporary Romance

SILHOUETTE BOOKS

ISBN 0-373-76365-4

MILLIONAIRE BOSS

This edition published by arrangement with Harlequin Books S.A.

® and TM are trademarks of Harlequin Books S.A., used under license. Trademarks indicated with ® are registered in the United States Patent and Trademark Office, the Canadian Trade Marks Office and in other countries.

Visit Silhouette at www.eHarlequin.com

**Printed in U.S.A.**

**Books by Peggy Moreland**

Silhouette Desire

*A Little Bit Country* #515
*Run for the Roses* #598
*Miss Prim* #682
*The Rescuer* #765
*Seven Year Itch* #837
*The Baby Doctor* #867
*Miss Lizzy's Legacy* #921
*A Willful Marriage* #1024
*\*Marry Me, Cowboy* #1084
*\*A Little Texas Two-Step* #1090
*\*Lone Star Kind of Man* #1096
*†The Rancher's Spittin' Image* #1156
*†The Restless Virgin* #1163
*†A Sparkle in the Cowboy's Eyes* #1168
*†That McCloud Woman* #1227
*Billionaire Bridegroom* #1244
*†Hard Lovin' Man* #1270
*‡Ride a Wild Heart* #1306
*‡In Name Only* #1313
*‡Slow Waltz Across Texas* #1315
*Groom of Fortune* #1336
*The Way to a Rancher's Heart* #1345
*Millionaire Boss* #1365

Silhouette Special Edition

*Rugrats and Rawhide* #1084

*Trouble in Texas
†Texas Brides
‡Texas Grooms

---

## PEGGY MORELAND

published her first romance with Silhouette in 1989 and continues to delight readers with stories set in her home state of Texas. Winner of the National Readers' Choice Award, a nominee for *Romantic Times* Reviewer's Choice Award and a finalist for the prestigious RITA Award, Peggy has appeared on the *USA Today* and Waldenbooks bestseller lists. When not writing, she enjoys spending time at the farm riding her quarter horse, Lo-Jump. She, her husband and three children make their home in Texas. You may write to Peggy at P.O. Box 1099, Florence, TX 76257-1099.

# One

It was the stuff romance novels were made of.

Man and Woman meet briefly during college, then go their separate ways after graduation.

Man dedicates his life to building a business and quickly establishes himself as a leader in the corporate world and as one of the most sought-after bachelors in the world.

Woman, having lost her heart to Man, resigns herself to being an old maid and devotes her life to keeping house for her widowed brother and caring for his three motherless children.

Ten years later Woman finds Man's classified ad for a secretary and applies for the job, certain that it is destiny that she has found the advertisement at the precise moment when she's decided her brother and his children have become too dependent on her and she needs to create a life of her own, separate from them.

Reunion takes place, where Man declares his undying love for Woman, and they live happily ever after.

Penny Rawley would have laughed at the clichéd plot and the pathetic heroine with her terminal case of unrequited love, if it wasn't her own life she was reflecting on…well, except for that last scene, the one with the reunion and happily-ever-after. That particular drama had yet to be played out.

But it would soon, she thought, glancing uneasily at the elevator doors opposite her desk. Would he recognize her when he arrived? she wondered nervously. Would he remember the young college coed who had typed his term papers for him ten years ago?

Odd as it seemed, though she'd worked for Erik Thompson for almost a month, she had yet to meet with him face-to-face…at least, not in the recent past. He had been on a business trip in Japan when Eleanor Hilloughby, the secretary whom Penny had replaced, had hired Penny for the job. A dear, sweet lady, Eleanor had claimed she was retiring to spend more time with her grandchildren—though Penny suspected the woman might well be, at this very moment, cheerfully weaving baskets in some insane asylum and not doting on her grandchildren as she'd professed.

After less than a month in Erik's employ, Penny was convinced that anyone who worked directly for the man was a prime candidate for a frontal lobotomy. He was disorganized, self-absorbed and communicated with his employees as if they were nothing but machines.

She huffed a breath at the reminder of the hundreds

of e-mails he'd blasted to her computer from the far
corners of the world. Nothing but fragments, the lot
of them. Clusters of words thrown together without
heed for syntax, spelling or punctuation. She found
deciphering them as tedious as unraveling a secret
code.

But what irked her more was that not *once,* in any
of the e-mails he'd sent to her, had he commented on
the change in his office staff or referred to her directly
in any way. Each post he'd sent was addressed to
mysecretary@cybercowboy.com. For all he'd indicated, Penny could be a monkey sitting behind what
was once Mrs. Hilloughby's desk, gleefully eating ba-
nanas while handling all his business and personal af-
fairs.

She told herself that it didn't matter, that the lack
of remembrance didn't hurt. Just because she remembered Erik, didn't mean that he should remember her,
as well. After all, she was Penny Rawley, poster child
for wallflowers worldwide. Plain. Forgettable. Invisible. Whereas, he was *the* Erik Thompson. Computer
genius. Entrepreneur extraordinaire. The most sought-
after bachelor in Texas, if not the world. The self-
proclaimed lawman who rode through cyber space on
bandwidth rather than a horse, packing a keyboard instead of a six-shooter as he tracked down criminals in
the relatively new frontier known as the Internet.

But it did hurt, she admitted, blinking back an unexpected rush of tears. If he didn't recognize her when
he arrived, or even acknowledge in some way that
he'd once made her acquaintance, she feared she'd die
of a broken heart…or, at the very least, suffer extreme
humiliation.

To heck with her date with destiny, she told herself,

already reaching for the purse she'd tucked within the kneehole space of her desk. She would quit. Leave before he arrived. Spare herself the heartbreak and humiliation. She'd find a new job. One with a lesser-known company, a less-infamous owner. One where she had no past connection with her employer.

Just as she stood, purse in hand, prepared to make a hasty exit, the elevator dinged, signaling its arrival on the executive floor. Trapped, with no escape left to her, she watched, frozen, as the doors slid silently open and the car's single male occupant stepped out. The man carried a briefcase in one hand and held a thick sheaf of papers before his face with the other.

She slid her gaze down his body, noting the black T-shirt with Cyber Cowboy emblazoned across its front, the faded jeans that hugged slim hips, the long, muscular legs whose long, sure strides brought him ever closer to her desk. She dragged her gaze from the tips of scuffed cowboy boots crafted from an unidentifiable exotic skin and back up to the coal-black hair that curled damply on his forehead and over his ears.

*Erik Thompson?* she asked herself in bewilderment. She'd expected him to have changed over the years, to have incorporated a more polished style, one that befit his current status and wealth. A three-piece, custom-made silk suit, Italian loafers, a gold Rolex watch. *Something* to attest to his success. But he hadn't changed at all! He still dressed like a down-on-his-luck cowboy, just as he had when she'd first met him in college ten years before.

Without lifting his gaze from the report he studied, he passed by her desk and mumbled a one-word directive for coffee.

She slowly turned her head, following his unflag-

ging progress toward his open office door. Her gaze
drifted from the dark hair that curled against the neck-
band of his T-shirt, down a broad back and tapered
waist to his buttocks and a frayed tear just below his
hip pocket. Her breath snagged in her lungs and
burned there as a strip of black silk appeared in the
narrow slit. Oh, my God! she thought, heat flooding
her face. Black silk briefs. He wears *black silk briefs!*
Her purse slipped from suddenly weak fingers and
dropped to the carpet with a soft thud at her feet.

Seemingly oblivious to the sound of her purse dropping or the lustful stare that monitored his movements,
he stepped inside his office, hooked the worn heel of
a cowboy boot around the bottom edge of the door
and gave it a shove. The door slammed shut between
them, the sound as sharp and startling as the report of
a gun, making Penny jump.

She placed a hand over her heart and sank weakly
down onto her chair. "Oh, my God," she murmured,
then said again more slowly, "Oh...my...God."

She wasn't sure how long she sat there, staring at
the closed door, an image of the man on the other side
filling her mind, her pulse thundering at the erotic visions that built, before his voice boomed from the
other side, "Where's my coffee!"

She hesitated, remembering her earlier decision to
leave, then bolted to her feet. *I'll give it a couple more
days,* she promised herself as she poured coffee into
the thick ceramic mug that Mrs. Hilloughby had indicated was his favorite. *Then, if I find him impossible
to work with, I'll quit.*

She snatched the itinerary from the printer as she
raced by her desk, but forced herself to pause outside
his door and take a deep breath, before knocking. Not

hearing a response, she opened the door and peeked inside.

He was seated behind the desk opposite her, the heels of his hands pressed against his temples, studying the report he'd dropped between his braced elbows. Sunshine streamed through the plate glass window behind him, creating a golden halo of sorts for a fallen angel.

At eighteen she'd thought Erik Thompson the best looking and sexiest man she'd ever met, and nothing she saw now changed that earlier opinion. Then, as now, he projected an image of strength, self-confidence, an intellectual intensity that merely hinted at the sharpness of a brilliant mind, an impatience to conquer the world and claim it as his own...and an inborn sexuality that turned her insides to warm, spun honey.

Granted, she had to look beyond his rough appearance to see those traits and experience that thrill. It seemed he still had an aversion to a comb and razor, she thought dreamily, as she skimmed her gaze over the damp curls that drooped endearingly over his forehead, the dark stubble that shadowed his jaw.

As she stared, he dragged a weary hand down his face, flipped a page, then returned the hand to his temple, as if he needed it to support the weight of his head. He's exhausted, she realized with a stab of sympathy, then just as quickly wondered at the cause of his fatigue.

Remembering his demand for coffee and suspecting his need for the stimulating caffeine was real rather than ego generated, she crossed to his desk. "Good morning, Mr. Thompson," she said, deciding the formal greeting more appropriate—especially since he hadn't seemed to recognize her. "How was your trip to Japan?"

His attention riveted on the report, he muttered something unintelligible and held out a hand. His response was so much like her brother's grumpy morning greetings to her, she was taken aback. Were all men alike? she wondered incredulously. Did they all take for granted that their needs would be met without a thought or a care for the person who was fulfilling those needs?

Determined to make him acknowledge her presence, she set the mug on his desk just out of his reach and took a step back. Folding her arms beneath her breasts, she pursed her lips and waited, tapping the itinerary furiously against her forearm.

After a moment he glanced up, his gaze snagging on the abandoned mug without ever making it to hers. Frowning slightly, he hooked a finger in its handle and shifted his gaze back to the report as he took the first cautious sip. "You the new secretary?"

Penny rolled her eyes. Even in conversation he seemed to communicate in sentence fragments, though she didn't need to struggle to decode *this* particular message. His meaning was all too clear and proved what she'd already suspected.

He didn't remember her.

But she didn't die of a broken heart, as she'd feared she might. Nor did she suffer even a shred of humiliation. Instead a slow fury burned its way through her. "Yes," she said, and thrust out a hand, determined to make him touch her, prove to him that she was a human being and not one of his complicated computer systems. "Penny Rawley."

He glanced up, met her gaze briefly, then dropped

his gaze to her hand. His frown deepening, he set aside his mug, gave her hand a quick pump, then released it. "Mrs. H. show you the ropes?" he asked, infuriating her further by turning a page of the report and continuing to read, instead of focusing his attention on her.

"Yes. She was very thorough."

"Took care of all the details in my life. Personal and business. Expect you to do the same."

"She made my duties quite clear."

One corner of his mouth tilted upward in what appeared to be a fond smile. The effect on her system was devastating.

"Yeah. I'm sure she did." He glanced up and met her gaze, those bedroom-blue eyes of his turning assessing as he let his gaze drift slowly down her front. It was all she could do to keep from patting self-consciously at the sensible bun she'd styled her long hair into, or tugging at the hem of her conservatively cut skirt. She held her breath, waiting for some sort of reaction from him, an indication that he remembered her.

When he merely shifted his attention back to his report, the breath sagged out of her, right along with all her wishful dreams. Disheartened, she placed the papers she held on his desk. "I've prepared your weekly itinerary. If you'll review it, I can answer any questions you might have."

Without looking up, he dragged the itinerary across the top of the report he'd been reading and scanned the first page while slowly sipping his coffee. He flipped quickly through the long list of appointments, then swept the itinerary aside and focused on the report again. "Cancel 'em."

Her brows shot up at the unexpected command. "Cancel them?" she repeated in surprise.

"Yeah. Leaving for California this afternoon. Gone for at least a week."

She stared, thinking of all the calls she'd have to make, the egos and tempers she'd surely have to soothe when she informed the individuals that *the* Erik Thompson would be unable to meet with them as previously scheduled.

He glanced up, his brows drawing together in a frown of impatience when he saw that she still stood opposite his desk. "Was there something else you needed?"

She backed toward the door. "W-well, no," she stammered. "Unless, of course, you have any other instructions for me."

He waved a hand, hastening her exit. "No." He swung his legs up, planting his boot heels on the polished surface of his desk, and reared back in his chair, holding the report before his face. "Not at the moment."

Erik lowered the report to peer at the door his secretary closed behind her.

A mouse, he thought in disgust as the door snapped shut with a quiet, cautious click. A prim and proper, red-headed, scared-of-her-shadow mouse. What the hell was Mrs. H. thinking when she hired a woman like that to take her place as his secretary?

Knowing there was only one way to find out, he pushed back his chair and strode from his office.

His new secretary—the mouse, as he'd already dubbed her—glanced up from her desk as he passed by.

"Where are you going?" she asked in surprise.

"Out."

"But you just got here!"

He ignored her and stepped onto the elevator, punching the button for the ground floor.

Twenty minutes later he was standing on the back stoop of his former secretary's house, waiting impatiently for her to respond to his knock.

When she did, he brushed past her. "Who's the mouse?"

"Mouse?" she repeated in confusion, closing the door behind him. "You mean the new secretary I hired for you?"

He pulled out a chair from the table and sat down. "Yeah. Her. What's the deal?"

She seated herself in the chair next to his. "You've met her, then," she said, looking pleased with herself.

"Yeah. And she's a mouse. What were you thinking? She'll never work out."

"But she's perfect," she insisted, as if surprised by his assessment. "Very organized, extremely intelligent, loyal to a fault. Plus, she's single and more than willing to work the odd hours your schedule demands."

"She's a mouse," he repeated disagreeably. "She'll never be able to stand up to the pressures of this job."

"You mean she'll never be able to withstand your temper tantrums."

He frowned at the reprimand in her tone and snatched up a salt shaker, narrowing an eye at it as he turned it in his hand. "That, too," he muttered, reluctant to admit that his former secretary had hit the nail on the head.

"Then maybe you ought to learn to control your

temper," she suggested, sounding more like a mother than a former employee.

Erik glanced over at her and set down the shaker, unable to suppress the half smile her scolding drew. God, but he was going to miss the old girl. "Why don't you give up on this retirement nonsense and come back to work for me? You know as well as I do that no one can replace you."

"Can't. My grandchildren need me."

"*I* need you," he argued. "Those rugrats have their own mothers to take care of them. I only have you."

"You're a big boy," she was quick to remind him, "and more than capable of taking care of yourself."

He let her argument pass without comment, allowing the silence to stretch out between them. He knew it was the right tactic when she began to wring her hands.

"When was the last time you ate?" she asked uneasily.

"Can't remember. At least a day. Maybe two."

"Erik Thompson!" she cried, and pushed herself from the table. "For heaven's sake," she fussed as she bustled about, setting a griddle on the stove and turning on a burner beneath it. "A man needs food to keep up his strength."

"Yeah, I know," he replied, smiling smugly. "That's why I need you."

She pursed her lips and gave him her best you're-not-fooling-me-for-a-minute-young-man look over her shoulder, then turned her attention to pouring pancake batter over the griddle.

Chuckling, Erik reared back in his chair and hooked his thumbs in the waist of his jeans as he glanced around the cozy kitchen. God, but he loved this room with its never-ending supply of mouthwatering aromas, ridiculous clutter of useless knickknacks, the jumble of artwork and pictures that papered the refrigerator door. He figured he'd spent more time at this table and in this room than he had in those of his childhood home, a fact that spoke volumes about his relationship with his parents.

"Have you heard anything more from Boy Wonder?" she asked as she flipped a pancake.

Erik frowned, reminded of the irritating and mysterious hacker that jumped from machine to machine and server to server, continuing to elude Erik. "Yeah. A couple of times. He's still around, slipping in back doors and into systems where he has no business."

"Has he done any damage?"

"None that I can determine. I figure he's due to do something big soon, though. He's been hanging around way too long."

"You'll catch him," she told him confidently.

"Damn straight," he muttered, irritated that the hacker had thus far managed to dodge the traps he'd set for him.

"She'll do a fine job."

He glanced up, mentally thrown off balance by the quick change in topic. Then, realizing she was referring to his new secretary, he scowled and pushed back, giving her room to set a plate in front of him. "Not as good as you."

She smiled, obviously pleased by the compliment as she sank down on the chair next to his. She placed a hand over his, her smile turning wistful. "I'm grateful for the job you offered me after Red died. I honestly don't know what I would've done, if not for you."

Reminded of the death five years earlier of the man who had been more a father to him than his own father ever had been, Erik firmed his lips against the emotion that crowded his throat. He turned his hand over and gripped his fingers around hers. "Red was a good man. The best."

Her eyes filled with tears. "He would be so proud of the work you're doing."

"He gave me my first chance. Taught me everything he knew."

"Yes, and he'd be even prouder to know that you took that knowledge and continued his work."

"*We* continued it," he argued, reminding her that she was very much a part of the work he'd carried on after her husband's death.

She laughed and gave his hand a squeeze before releasing it. "And I enjoyed every minute of it. But it's time for me to enter the next stage of my life, that of doting grandmother."

"You'll be bored out of your mind in a month's time, I guarantee it."

"No," she told him, and lifted her apron's skirt to dab the telltale tears from her eyes. "I'm really looking forward to spending time with my grandbabies."

He braced his forearms on the table and leaned toward her, his expression growing earnest. "Then just go part-time at the office. There's no reason why you can't continue to work for me and spend time with your grandchildren, too."

Chuckling, she shook her head. "You're just afraid that if I retire completely I won't cook for you anymore."

He scowled, but picked up his fork. "That's not it at all. I need you, Mrs. H. We're a team."

"And you and Penny will make a good team, too."
She smiled and placed a hand on his cheek. "Give her
a chance," she urged gently. "You'll see. Penny Rawley is exactly the woman you need in your life."

Hours later Erik was still scowling, wondering what
Mrs. H. had meant by that last comment.

*Penny Rawley is exactly the woman you need in
your life.*

Was the old girl playing matchmaker? he wondered
as he glanced over at his secretary, who sat before a
computer terminal at the end of his credenza, tran-
scribing from tapes the data he'd recorded during his
meetings in Japan.

He quickly looked away, discarding the troublesome thought. No, he told himself. Though Mrs. H.
had run roughshod over his life for more than fifteen
years, ever since Red had brought Erik home with him
the first time, and over Erik's office since her husband's death, she'd never once tried to fix him up with
a woman.

He glanced up again as his new secretary rose and
headed for her adjoining office. Her hand was on the
doorknob when he called out, "Hold up a sec."

Penny stopped, startled by her employer's barked
command, her heart seeming to stop, too. It leaped into
a pounding, joyous beat as she turned to face him, as
she was sure that he had at last remembered her.
"Yes?" she asked expectantly.

"Do you have any family?"

"Well...no," she replied, caught off guard by the
unexpected question. "Other than a brother, two
nieces and a nephew," she added prudently.

"Good." He spun his chair around and grabbed the

mouse next to his keyboard and began to scroll through a complicated table of computer codes. "'Cause you're going to California with me this afternoon."

Her eyes widened as she stared at the back of his head. "To California? With you?"

"Yeah. Go home and pack a bag. Throw in something fancy," he added.

She gulped a breath, trying to absorb the fact that she would be traveling with him. "Fancy?" she repeated dully.

"Yeah. You know. A cocktail dress or something."

"B-but why?"

His brows drew together as he found the information he was looking for and clicked on the accompanying file. "A black-tie thing," he mumbled. "Supposed to bring a date."

# Two

Suzy shoved Penny's suitcase aside and flopped down on her stomach on the bed, propping her chin on her hands. "I can't believe Erik didn't remember you."

Disappointed because he hadn't, Penny avoided Suzy's gaze. "It's been ten years," she reminded her friend.

"So what? It's been ten years for you, too, and you remembered him."

"Yes, but that's different."

Suzy rolled her eyes but—thankfully—let the comment pass without argument. Instead, she craned her neck and peered over the side of the suitcase, poking through the items Penny had already packed. "So how long will y'all be gone?"

"A week."

"Are you planning on jumping his bones?"

Penny whirled from her closet. "Suzy!"

Arching a brow, Suzy held up a plastic case, taunting Penny with the damning evidence she'd found. "Why else would you have started taking the Pill?"

Her cheeks flaming, Penny snatched the packet of birth control pills from her friend's hand and shoved it back into her suitcase, burying it beneath a stack of underwear. "That's none of your business. Besides, I started them over a month ago." Just about the time she'd applied for the job as Erik's secretary, she thought but didn't say.

Chuckling, Suzy sat up, plumping pillows at the headboard before sinking back against them. "Just trying to help you face the facts."

"If you want to be helpful," Penny replied irritably, "you can tell me what I should wear to a black-tie affair."

"What are your choices?"

Penny turned to study the row of clothes hanging neatly in her closet. "Well, there's the floral dress that I wore Easter Sunday three years ago," she offered, then glanced at Suzy. "You know. The calf-length dress with cap-sleeves and Puritan-style collar?"

Groaning, Suzy covered her face with her hands. "Please tell me you're not seriously considering wearing that old thing?"

"What's wrong with the floral dress?"

"Nothing, if you were going to be herding a gaggle of toddlers at an Easter egg hunt. Jeez, Pen," she complained. "You gotta stop dressing like somebody's mother. Think bold. Daring. Go for shock value. I guarantee you, if you do, not a man in the room will be able to take his eyes off you. Not even the Cyber Cowboy himself."

Penny turned to stare at the clothes hanging in her

closet, all of which seemed more appropriate for a PTA meeting at one of her nieces' or nephew's schools than for a cocktail party escorted by Erik Thompson.

Not that he would notice her, anyway, she thought, swallowing back a swell of tears.

"I don't have anything else," she said, sniffing as she dragged the floral dress from its hanger. "It'll just have to do."

Suzy vaulted from the bed. "Then let's go shopping. We'll buy you something sinfully expensive. Something totally outrageous that will have Erik Thompson's eyes bugging out of his head."

Tempted, Penny glanced at the bedside clock, and the tears pushed to her eyes. "There isn't time. I have to meet him at the office parking lot at five." She swept a hand across her cheeks, then carefully folded the floral dress and placed it in her suitcase. "This will just have to do."

Suzy moved to stand beside her and slipped an arm around her shoulders. "The dress'll do fine. And so will you," she added, giving Penny a reassuring squeeze. Drawing away, she sighed as she scooped her purse from the foot of the bed. "I guess I'd better go so you can finish packing. Call me the minute you get back in town."

"I will."

"You'd better," Suzy warned as she headed for the bedroom door. "I want to hear every intimate detail. Oh, and Penny?"

Penny turned to look at her. "What?"

"Don't forget to take your pills."

Erik lounged against the hood of his truck, his arms folded over his chest and his buttocks braced against the grill guard, watching as his new secretary steered her beige sedan into her assigned space in the building's underground parking garage. The vehicle was as plain and nondescript as its owner, he thought, with a woeful shake of his head.

What was Mrs. H. thinking when she hired the woman? he wondered again. Penny Rawley was a mouse, afraid of her own shadow. The first time he lost his temper—which, he admitted, he was prone to do on occasion—she'd probably run from his office, bawling. And he didn't have the time or patience to deal with a crybaby.

Scowling, he watched her flip up her sun visor, eject a cassette tape from the player on the dash, then carefully slip the tape into its plastic case and tuck it neatly into the console. Her movements were as methodical as a pilot's, clicking off controls after a landing…which wasn't a bad thing, he reflected grudgingly. Erik appreciated order. Not that he managed to ever create it on his own. But that's what secretaries were for, right? Hadn't Mrs. H. always taken care of all the little details of his life, allowing him the freedom and time to focus on the bigger, more important issues?

Damn straight she had, he thought, swallowing back a lump of emotion. He was going to miss the old girl. She had possessed a sixth sense for determining his mood and anticipating his needs, and had managed for the most part to ignore his temper tantrums…but was unafraid to give him a good tongue lashing when she felt he deserved one.

And now he was stuck with a damn mouse, he thought irritably as he watched his new secretary twist around inside her car to collect something from the back seat.

Her hair was still wound up in that old-maid bun he'd noticed at the office that morning, and she was dressed in the same utilitarian suit, with that damn fussy bow tied prissily beneath her chin.

A week, he thought with a sigh as he heaved himself away from his truck and headed for her car. He'd be lucky if he didn't die of boredom after the first day.

When he reached the side of her car, he bent over, bracing his hands on his knees to place his face level with the open window. "Ready?"

Before he knew what was happening, he found himself staring at the business end of a small canister of mace. A mouse fending off a man-eating lion. The image that popped into his mind was ridiculous enough to be comical.

"Please don't shoot," he deadpanned. "I'll go peacefully."

She sagged weakly, then clamped her lips together and reached for the window's handle, rolling the glass up between them with quick jerks of her hand. After snatching her shoulder bag from the passenger seat, she shoved open the door. "You startled me," she accused.

He arched a brow, surprised by the unexpected display of temper. "Didn't mean to," he said, stepping out of her way. "Was just going to offer to help you with your luggage."

She headed for the rear of her car, her nose in the air. "I can manage on my own, thank you."

She stabbed the key into the lock, gave it a furious twist, then flung up the lid. Their hands brushed and their heads bumped as they both reached for the bag she'd stored inside. She leaped back, clutching her hand against her chest, as if stung.

Scowling, he pulled her bag from the trunk. "Over there," he said, with a jerk of his head toward his truck, then slapped a palm against the trunk's lid, slamming it down.

She drew the strap of her purse to her shoulder and turned, but stopped before she'd taken a full step, her eyes going wide.

He pressed a hand against the small of her back. "What's the matter?" he asked, giving her a nudge to put her into motion. "Never seen a truck before?"

She sidestepped just enough to escape his touch. "Of course I've seen a truck," she replied, sounding flustered. "I grew up on a ranch. I just never considered that you would drive one."

He tossed her bag into the back, then opened the passenger door and shot her a wink as he held it open. "No true cowboy would be caught dead driving anything else."

When she continued to hesitate, nervously eyeing the gaping distance between the ground and the running board created by the six-inch lift he'd added to the truck's original design, he realized the cause of her concern. Short of hiking her skirt up around her waist, there was no way she was going to negotiate the climb.

Though he thought that scenario might be worth observing, he resolved her problem by wrapping an arm around her waist and swinging her up. She squealed as he swept her from the ground, then clung to him as he planted her conservative little pumps on the floorboard and her fanny on the passenger seat.

Dusting off his hands, he took a step back. "Comfortable?" he asked, trying hard not to smile.

She stared at him, her green eyes wide and unblinking, her face pale but for two bright spots of color high on her cheeks. A wisp of carrot-red hair had escaped her bun and now brushed her temple. A sense of déjà vu swept over him. Had he seen those eyes before, that face? Had he enacted this scene before?

A frown puckered his brow as he narrowed an eye at her. "Have we—"

She tore her gaze from his and turned to face the front. "Quite comfortable," she replied, cutting him off. "Thank you."

Erik frowned a moment longer, then lifted his shoulder and headed for the driver's side of his truck.

Penny stole a peek at Erik, who sat slumped in the seat next to hers, his head tipped back, his eyes closed, his lips slightly parted in sleep. Though the private jet's cabin was dimly lit, the overhead reading lamp and the glow from his laptop computer screen provided enough light to illuminate features she'd always considered too perfect to be human.

Taking advantage of this rare opportunity to study him unawares, she leaned for a closer look. He hasn't changed all that much, she noted. The squint lines fanning from the corners of his eyes were a little deeper than she remembered and his cheeks were a little more lean, but basically he looked the same as the memory she'd kept locked away in her heart for the past ten years.

She caught her lower lip between her teeth, wondering what he would say if she were to tell him that she'd fantasized about him throughout the years, weaving dreams about him that made her blush even now to think about them.

He'd probably laugh, she thought, swallowing back the disappointment. He'd never given her a moment's notice in college, treating her much as he did now, as if she were nothing but a robot programmed to do his work. Then her purpose had been to earn him an A in English. Now it was to take care of all the little details in his business and personal life.

*So what exactly is it about this man that you find so irresistible?*

Shying away from the question, she plucked a piece of lint from the sleeve of his T-shirt...then, unable to resist, let her fingers linger on the gentle swell of biceps. The memory of him scooping her up into his arms and plunking her into his truck, settled like a heavy mist over her mind and her heart. Unconsciously she let her fingers drift down his sleeve, shivering when she encountered warm flesh. Then, realizing what she was doing, she snatched back her hand and squeezed her eyes shut.

*Oh, Lord,* she cried silently. *I'll never survive a whole week without jumping him like some sex-starved nymphomaniac!*

In spite of her determination to do otherwise, she stole another peek at him and had to grip her hands over the armrests to keep from reaching out and brushing back the endearing lock of hair that drooped over his forehead.

He's too handsome, she thought, feeling the panic rising higher. Too worldly, too sexy...too everything!

And she was plain-as-a-copper-penny Penny Rawley, a dried-up old maid who'd barely ventured farther than fifty miles from the ranch she'd grown up on.

Disheartened by the reminder, she lifted a hand to

turn off the overhead light, not trusting herself to look at him any longer without touching him again.

But just as her finger brushed the light's button, an electronic alarm beeped shrilly on his laptop computer. Frozen in place by the chilling sound, she watched the screen flash red.

Erik bolted upright, knocking his forehead against the hand she still held aloft. He blinked twice, then shoved her arm from in front of his face and grabbed for his laptop, drawing it to the edge of the portable desk.

"I didn't touch it," she said quickly, fearing the dark scowl that creased his brow was an indication that he thought she'd done something to harm his precious computer. "I swear. I just reached up to turn off your light."

"It's him," he muttered, ignoring her, his eyes riveted on the screen.

"Him?" she repeated, turning to stare at the screen. "Him who?"

Eyes narrowed, his fingers fairly flying over the keyboard, he replied, "Boy Wonder."

She stared, watching as window after window popped into view, the information that flashed on each as foreign to her as Erik's reference to Boy Wonder.

"He's just down the street." He set his jaw as he increased the size of one window and scrolled through the garbled lines of data registered there.

"Down the street?" she repeated, wondering if he realized they were presently flying 30,000 feet above the ground.

"From the office," he snapped impatiently, then swore and slammed a fist down on the edge of the portable desk, making the laptop, as well as Penny, jump. "He's gone," he said, then swore again. "That sneaky hacker slipped through the cracks again."

Frightened by his anger, she asked uneasily, "Who is Boy Wonder?"

"If I knew *who* he was," he growled, "I wouldn't be sitting here listening to you yap. I'd be hauling his butt to jail."

Resenting his contemptuous reply to what she considered a simple and justifiable question, Penny flounced around in her seat and slapped her arms across her chest. "Well, excuse me. It isn't as if I'm aware of every detail of your life and business. I've only worked for your company a month, you know."

Erik whipped his head around, prepared to lambast his secretary...but when he saw her face, his scathing retort dried up in his mouth.

Those were tears in her eyes, he realized, his stomach clenching at the sight of them. Big alligator-size tears that looked as if they might overflow her eyes and slide down her cheeks at any moment. A twinge of something close to guilt—an emotion Erik rarely indulged in—pricked at him and he tore his gaze from her.

Not your fault, he told himself as he shut down his laptop. She's a mouse. A crybaby. Totally incapable of handling the stress her job entailed.

"Cry and you're fired," he warned as he shoved the laptop under his seat. "I won't have a crybaby working for me."

Penny turned her head again, this time away to face the opposite bank of windows, blinking furiously. "I'm not a crybaby."

"Could've fooled me."

She graced him with the coldest, most damning look

she could muster under the circumstances. "I'm not a crybaby," she repeated tersely. "But *you*, on the other hand, are undoubtedly the rudest, most self-possessed, most linguistically challenged man I've ever met."

"Never said I wasn't," he replied easily, then frowned. "Linguistically challenged? What the hell is that supposed to mean?"

Jutting her chin, she smoothed the hem of her skirt over her knees. "My point exactly."

His frown deepening, he shoved back his seat and closed his eyes. "You are, too, a crybaby," he muttered, then held up a hand in warning, as if anticipating a comeback from her. "I'm going to sleep," he informed her. "And I'd advise you to do the same. We've got a lot of work to do once we reach California."

Moaning softly, Penny sat up straighter in her chair and pressed a hand to her lower back, arching against it as she tried to ease the dull ache there. After more than six hours sitting before a monitor, entering and tracking data for her employer, her eyes burned from the strain of staring at a glowing screen, and every muscle in her body screamed from sitting in the inappropriately designed chair.

Erik certainly hadn't exaggerated when he'd warned her that they'd have a lot of work to do once they reached California, she thought wearily.

Sighing, she rose and crossed to the wet bar in the hotel's penthouse suite in search of something to drink. "Would you like a soda?" she asked. "Or something to eat? We never got around to eating lunch," she reminded him.

When he didn't respond, she glanced his way. He

sat slumped on the overstuffed sofa as he had all day, his cowboy boots propped on the coffee table, his laptop balanced on jean-clad thighs. His forehead looked like a freshly plowed field, the furrows that ran across it deep and wavy, a testament to the level and intensity of his concentration.

The man is a machine, she thought in disgust, a suspicion she'd formed before their trip to California, but now knew for a fact.

They'd arrived in California a little after ten the night before and were at their hotel by eleven, where she'd discovered to her dismay that he intended that they share a suite. She hadn't had time to recover from the shock of that nerve-warping discovery before Erik had hustled her onto a glass elevator and to a penthouse on the hotel's uppermost floor.

Once there she lost her ability to speak when confronted with the elaborately appointed and spacious suite—which, thankfully, she'd discovered consisted of a living area and two large bedrooms, each with its own private and luxurious bath. Erik hadn't shared her starry-eyed fascination with the suite's opulence and its ceiling-to-floor view of San Diego's skyline, or her desire to explore. Instead he had immediately mumbled a curt good-night and gone straight to his room and to bed.

Disappointed, Penny had gone to her room, as well. But when she'd awakened that morning, she'd found herself alone in the suite—though, not for long. She'd barely had time to shower and don a fresh suit before Erik had returned, carrying a briefcase filled with a thick stack of reports. Without a word of greeting or explanation as to his whereabouts, he'd given her clipped orders to enter the data from the reports into a computer he'd set up for her on the suite's only desk.

They'd worked silently and without a break ever since.

Sighing again, she chose a can of juice for her employer, poured it into a glass, then selected some fresh fruit, cheese and crackers from the basket on the bar and arranged them on a plate.

"Here," she said, placing the snack on the coffee table beside his propped boots. "Eat."

When he didn't respond, she drew in a frustrated breath. "Mr. Thompson!"

He jumped, swore, then glared up at her. "What?"

"Food," she said and pointed to the plate. "Now eat before you collapse from lack of nourishment."

He scowled and turned his face back to the screen. "Not hungry."

Wondering why life seemed to always link her with grumpy, sour-faced men who didn't have the good sense to take care of themselves, Penny snatched the laptop computer from his thighs.

"Hey!" he cried, dropping his feet to the floor and sitting up. "What do you think you're doing?"

"Taking care of you," she replied, "just as Mrs. Hilloughby instructed me to do. Though I can see it will be a thankless job," she added with more than a little resentment. She set the computer out of his reach, then pointed a finger at the plate. "Now eat," she ordered.

Scowling, he snatched up the plate and fell back against the sofa. He stuffed a strawberry into his mouth and smashed it between his teeth. "Satisfied?" he asked, dashing a hand over his chin to catch a stream of juice that leaked from the corner of his mouth.

With a sniff, she turned for the bar to make a snack for herself. "Only when the plate is clean."

Erik narrowed an eye at his secretary as she sank down onto a chair opposite the sofa, primly balancing her plate over pressed-together knees.

"What did you do before you came to work for me? No," he said, holding up a hand before she could respond. "Let me guess. An army nurse? A nun in an all-girl school? A prison guard for a chain gang? A marine drill sergeant?"

She offered him a tight smile. "Funny. But, no, I was none of those things. After graduating from college, I was employed at a local bank, serving as the bank president's secretary. I resigned about three years ago to work for my brother."

"Doing what? Breaking kneecaps for him? Kicking puppies? Stealing old ladies' canes?"

Though his suggestions were outrageous enough to be humorous, Penny refused to dignify his sarcasm with a smile. "My duties included housekeeping, cooking for a family of five and caring for my nieces and nephew."

He bit a chunk off a wedge of cheese. "Why'd you leave?"

Uncomfortable with his close scrutiny, as well as his question, she lifted a shoulder. "My brother is a widower and depended on me too much, leaving the care of his children entirely up to me. If I'd stayed, he would have continued to ignore them." She lifted a shoulder again. "So I left."

"Bet your brother was plenty ticked at you for leaving him in a bind."

She stiffened, reminded of Jase's angry phone call when he'd returned to the ranch and found her gone and a new nanny in her place. "I didn't leave him in a bind," she stated defensively. "I hired a woman as my replacement. A very capable woman, I might add, who immediately won the children over with her cheerful disposition and youthful exuberance."

"Cheerful disposition and youthful exuberance?" He snorted a laugh and popped a grape into his mouth. "Who'd you hire? Mary Poppins?"

Irritated by his contemptuous remark, she ignored him and nibbled on a slim wedge of Gouda she'd selected from the variety of gourmet cheeses she'd placed on her plate.

He shook his head and popped the last strawberry into his mouth. "Should've stayed with your brother," he said as he set the plate aside and reclaimed his laptop. "No kid deserves to have a stranger dumped on 'em…even if the alternative *is* being saddled with a frumpy old aunt who wouldn't know fun if it bit her square on the butt."

*Frumpy old aunt?*

Numb, Penny could only stare, his description of her smacking at an already bruised self-esteem.

She rose quickly, tears stinging her eyes, and crossed to the bar, furiously blinking them back, not wanting to give him the opportunity to call her a cry-baby again. She dumped the remains of her snack into the waste basket, rinsed off her plate, then grabbed her purse from the bar and headed for the door.

At the sound of her leaving, he glanced up. "Hey! Where do you think you're going?"

"For a walk," she replied, trying her best to keep the tears from her voice.

"But we've got that black-tie thingamajig at seven."

"I'll be back before then," she promised, then quickly closed the door behind her before he saw her tears and knew how much his tactless—if accurate—description of her had hurt.

Penny walked down the street, her chin bumping dejectedly against her chest, her gaze on the blurred tips of her black pumps. She wanted to despise Erik for the cruel things he'd said about her but found she couldn't. Not when he was right. She *was* frumpy. And she feared she wasn't much fun, either.

But how could she be fun, she cried in silent frustration, or even know what it was, when she'd never been allowed to have any while growing up? After their parents' death, Jase had assumed guardianship of her, and if Erik thought Penny didn't know what fun was, then he should meet her brother, Jase, the epitome of the glowering wielder of the proverbial whip.

She caught her lower lip between her teeth, feeling a stab of guilt for her less-than-charitable thoughts toward a brother who had sacrificed so much for her. Life hadn't exactly been kind to either of them, she reflected sadly. Their parents' death had forced Jase to drop out of college and return home to take care of Penny and run the family ranch. And ranch life left little time for fun. Penny knew, because for years she'd worked right alongside her brother.

And when her friends had gone off to college to kick up their heels and spread their wings a little, Penny had remained at home, commuting from their ranch to Austin each day to take courses at the University of Texas. And with Jase, by that time, saddled with the responsibilities of his own growing family, Penny had felt obligated to help finance her education by typing term papers for other students and offering tutoring on the side. Between the long commute, a full load of classes each semester, evenings spent with her head buried in books and whatever hours left over in the day filled with typing term papers or tutoring some unmotivated jock, pitifully few hours remained in which to make new friends or pursue a social life.

No, she thought miserably as she dragged her feet to a stop before a shop's window display. Penny Rawley wouldn't know fun if it were to bite her square in the butt, just as Erik had suggested.

Fearing she would cry again if she allowed herself to think about the upsetting conversation any longer, she forced herself to focus on the items displayed in the window. Skimpy sundresses in varying shades of the rainbow draped headless mannequins with hourglass figures, while cropped tank tops danced from invisible strings above coordinating shorts that looked barely long enough to cover a woman's behind.

And superimposed over it all was Penny's reflection.

Slowly she focused on it. The sensible bun. The tailored blouse with its crisp bow tied neatly beneath her chin. The utilitarian suit jacket that hung loosely at her hips, hiding a figure that Penny wasn't even sure existed any more. The A-line skirt, its hem brushing modestly at her knees. She couldn't see any farther…but she didn't need to see more of her reflection to realize that *frump* fit her to a T.

Sickened by the reminder that Erik was right to label her a frump, she started to turn away but stopped and slowly turned back around. But she didn't have to be a frump, she told herself as she stared at her reflection. She could change. There was no reason she couldn't dress differently. Granted, she'd never bothered to stay abreast of current fashion trends. Had no need, not when her wardrobe was dictated by what was serviceable for ranch and housework. But that's what sales clerks were for, right? It was their job to stay on top of what was hot and what was not in the fashion industry. Surely she could trust one of them to help her make a few selections.

Remembering the black-tie affair that Erik expected her to attend with him at seven and the floral dress she'd brought to wear, she glanced at her watch. Two hours. She had two hours in which to recreate herself.

*Oh, Lord,* she prayed silently, *please let it be long enough to create a miracle.*

# Three

———

Penny knew she was late and that Erik would probably be furious with her. But she didn't care. She was too high, too pumped with excitement to care about anything, other than her new look.

Burdened with her purchases, she fumbled the card key for their hotel suite into the slot, pushed the toe of her shoe against the door, then hurried inside. "Mr. Thompson?" she called. "I'm back."

When she didn't hear a response, she headed straight for her bedroom, wincing when she saw a piece of paper taped to the door. After dumping her purchases on her bed, she removed the note and read: "Where the hell are you? Main ballroom. Now."

He hadn't even bothered signing his name.

Refusing to let his curt note rob her of her good mood, she tossed the paper over her shoulder and dived gleefully into the pile of purchases she'd dumped on the bed. Finding the clothing bag that covered her new dress, she held it up high…and her smile slowly faded.

*I can't do this,* she cried silently, panicking. *There's no way in the world I can possibly wear in public a dress made from scarcely more fabric than that of a man's oversize handkerchief.*

*Oh, yes, you can,* a voice insisted—a voice that sounded suspiciously like her friend Suzy's. *And you're going to make Erik Thompson's eyes pop right out of his head.*

Clutching the dress to her breasts, Penny headed for the bathroom, repeating under her breath a phrase from the story "The Little Engine that Could," which her niece Rachel loved Penny to read.

"I think I can, I think I can, I think I can."

Erik tipped back his head and drained the champagne from the glass, then plunked it down on the tray of a passing waiter. He glanced toward the ballroom's entrance for about the zillionth time since entering the room and swore under his breath when he still didn't see a sign of his missing secretary. Scowling, he stuffed his hands into the pockets of his tuxedo slacks and headed for the buffet table.

"Hey, Erik!"

Balancing a plate on his palm, Erik glanced over his shoulder and saw his old friend Buzz Kenney bearing down on him. Relieved to find a familiar face among a sea of strangers, he plucked another skewer of grilled shrimp from the tray. He used his teeth to drag one off its end, before dropping the skewer to his plate and turning to greet his friend. "How's it going, Buzz?"

"Can't complain." Buzz slapped a bear-like hand against Erik's back. "How 'bout you?"

Erik's eyes bugged as the force of Buzz's greeting made the shrimp he'd just swallowed hang in his throat. He gulped, swallowed hard, forcing it down, then slipped a finger behind his shirt's starched collar and craned his neck. "Fine," he croaked, "until you came along."

Buzz tossed his head back and boomed a laugh. "You always were a bit on the puny side."

Erik shot his friend a frown. "And you were always an overgrown bully."

"Now, Erik," Buzz chided. "Surely by now you've forgiven me for shoving you buck naked into the girl's locker room when we were in junior high?"

"Oh, I've forgiven you all right," Erik replied dryly. "I just haven't forgotten the incident. Nor will I."

Chuckling, Buzz draped a companionable arm along Erik's shoulders and turned to survey the room. "Mmm-mmm. Have you ever seen so many gorgeous babes gathered under one roof?"

Erik chose a bacon-wrapped mushroom from his plate and popped it into his mouth, not bothering to look up. "Yeah. One too many times."

Buzz clasped a hand over his heart. "Oh, man. Don't tell me the great Erik Thompson has lost his appetite for beautiful women?"

Erik lifted an indifferent shoulder. "If you've tasted one, you've tasted 'em all."

"Then you haven't been samplin' from the same buffets *I've* been feedin' from." He dug an elbow into Erik's ribs, then boomed another laugh when the dig sent Erik staggering sideways a step.

Frowning, Erik rubbed a hand over a rib he was sure would be sore the next day. "Why don't you go beat up on somebody else for a while?"

"And leave you all alone?" Grinning, Buzz folded his arms across his chest and rocked back on his heels, trolling the room with his gaze again. "Caught that pesky hacker yet that's been givin' you grief?"

Irritated by the reminder, Erik plucked a filled champagne glass from the tray of a passing waiter. "No." He tossed back half the bubbly liquid.

"Boy Wonder, isn't it?" Buzz asked, angling his head to look at Erik for confirmation.

"Boy Worrywart, would be more like it. The guy's becoming a royal pain in the ass, ducking in and out of systems, nosing around where he hasn't any business."

Buzz arched a thick brow, leveling a pointed look at Erik. "Sounds like a kid I used to know."

In spite of the years that separated him from his crimes, Erik felt the heat crawl up his neck. "Yeah, but I was just a kid. Didn't know any better."

"Maybe Boy Wonder's just a kid, too. His name suggests he might be."

Erik's frown deepened. "No kid is *that* good."

"You ought to know," Buzz replied, and turned his gaze back to the room. "You were the best." He puckered his lips in a silent whistle. "Whooee. Would you look at that?" He gave the points of his bow tie a gleeful tug. "Ultimate babe at three o'clock."

Erik rolled his eyes, amazed that a man Buzz's age still reverted to locker-room lingo when confronted with a good-looking woman. "Are your hormones always on red alert?"

Buzz grinned as he headed toward the redhead who

had caught his eye. "Wouldn't want 'em any other way."

In spite of himself, Erik found himself chuckling as he watched Buzz move in for the kill. He pitied the poor woman his buddy had zeroed in on. The woman didn't know it yet, but she didn't stand a snowball's chance in hell of resisting Buzz's killer charm. The man had more moves than a Ryder truck and more come-on lines than a drunk in a bar at closing time. Erik knew because he'd seen the man in action more times than he cared to remember.

Shaking his head, he started to turn for a second helping from the generous spread of hors d'oeuvres, but spun back, every muscle in his body tensed in denial.

No, he told himself as he stared at the woman smiling shyly up at Buzz. It couldn't be. He took a step toward the couple, but stopped, sure that he was wrong.

No, he told himself again. The hair color was right, but the style was all wrong. Mouse wore her hair twisted up in a tight, spinsterish bun, not swinging at shoulder length and mussed as if she'd gone a fast round in bed with an overly zealous lover. And there was no way in hell that woman's body could possibly belong to his secretary. Not that he had a clue what his secretary's figure looked like. Not when he'd seen her in nothing but those stupid, sexless suits favored by so many executive-type women.

In spite of his doubts, he found himself taking another step toward the couple. Then another. And another until he'd reached Buzz's side. He slapped a hand against his friend's back. "Hey, Buzz," he said, turning on a killer smile that he knew from experience most women found hard to resist. "Aren't you going to introduce me to your friend?"

"And chance losing her to a smooth talker like you? Man, I'm not that—"

Whatever else Buzz had to say on the subject was lost to Erik as the woman turned to fully face him. "Damn," he gasped weakly, bracing a hand against Buzz's arm for support as he found himself staring into all-too-familiar green eyes. He dragged his gaze from her face and down her front, nearly choking when he encountered the mounds of creamy flesh that the bustier-style bodice pushed above the dress's heart-shaped neckline. "Penny?" he asked, forcing his gaze back to her face. "Is that you?"

Though her smile remained in place, he saw the uncertainty in her eyes, recognized the level of nerves in the tremble of the fingers she smoothed down her thighs—thighs that the dress's brief hemline barely covered.

"Yes," she said, then caught her lower lip between her teeth and dropped her gaze, nearly making him groan at the provocativeness in the demure gesture. "I'm sorry I'm late," she murmured. "I was... detained." She peeked up at him through a web of lashes. "You aren't upset with me, are you?"

"Upset?" he repeated, when upset was much too mild a word to use to describe his earlier dark mood. "No," he lied. "I was just worried that you'd gotten lost or that something might have happened to you."

She laid a hand on his arm. "I'm so sorry to have worried you," she said with a contriteness that he would expect from the Penny he'd gotten to know over the last twenty-four hours. But he wasn't sure he knew who this new Penny was...or if he even liked the change.

He frowned, eyeing her suspiciously. "What'd you do to your hair?"

She caught a lock between her fingers and twisted self-consciously. "I had it cut this afternoon. Do you like it?"

He deepened his frown. "It's all right...I guess."

Her disappointment was instantaneous and blatantly obvious, even to a man as self-possessed as people claimed Erik to be.

Buzz stepped between the two. "I like your new hairstyle just fine," he assured Penny, then gallantly offered her his arm. "Now how 'bout that dance you promised me?"

Penny looked up at Buzz, her hesitancy to accept his invitation evident in her wide, green eyes. She glanced at Erik, then quickly away, and forced a smile as she slipped her arm through Buzz's. "I'd love to."

Erik stood where they had left him, watching the man he'd once considered his oldest and closest friend steer his secretary toward the dance floor. When they reached the area and Penny stepped into Buzz's arms, Erik whirled for the bar, muttering curses under his breath about playboys and innocent lambs being led to the slaughter.

It was well after midnight when Erik unlocked the door to their hotel suite and gestured impatiently for Penny to enter before him.

Her cheeks flushed with excitement, she swept past him on ridiculously high heels, trailing a provocative scent that had Erik lifting his nose and sniffing the air, in spite of his current disgust with his secretary.

She tossed a glittery purse the size of a small envelope onto the sofa, then spun, her hand clasped beneath her chin. "Wasn't that the most wonderful party!"

Disgusted by her exuberance—as well as by her behavior for the last couple of hours—Erik shrugged out of his tuxedo jacket and threw it toward the sofa. It landed on the floor about two feet shy of his mark. "It was all right," he muttered.

"All right?" she repeated, then laughed gaily and flung her arms wide. "I can't remember when I've had such a marvelous time. The orchestra was absolutely divine, and your friend, Buzz, such a skillful dancer. I've never swing danced before, but he was so patient with me, so kind to offer instruction."

Erik cut a glance at her, then frowned as he emptied the contents of his pockets onto the bar, resenting her good mood, but unsure why. "We're here to work," he reminded her. "Best you remember that."

Her eyes widened in alarm. "Oh, I haven't forgotten." She quickly stooped to scoop his jacket from the floor, then straightened, holding it against her chest as she smoothed the wrinkles from it.

But not before Erik had gotten another good look at the luscious mounds threatening to spill over the top of her dress.

He tore his gaze from the tempting sight and ducked behind the bar, suddenly finding himself in dire need of a drink. Selecting a miniature bottle of bourbon, he dumped its contents into a glass, started to add water, then decided against it and tossed the drink back, neat. He inhaled sharply as the bourbon hit the back of his throat, gulped it down, then hissed a breath as the liquor burned a path all the way to his stomach.

He glanced over to find Penny staring at him in horror.

"What?" he snapped impatiently.

"You aren't intending to get drunk, are you?"

He scowled and reached for another bottle. "Might. What's it to you, if I do?"

She took a step toward him, then stopped, hugging his jacket against her breasts. "Nothing. It's just that…well, you did say that we have a lot of work to do while we're here."

He dumped the bottle's contents into the glass, then lifted it, swirling the amber liquid lazily around the glass's sides as he met her gaze. "Don't worry about me. I can take care of myself. While *you*," he added, gesturing at her with the glass, "are going to require close supervision."

"Me!" she cried. "Whatever for?"

He tossed back half the bourbon, then dragged the back of his hand across his mouth, firming his lips against the heat that seared his throat. "You're like the country mouse who went to the big city. All wide-eyed innocence when confronted with the big bad wolf."

Her brow pleated in confusion. "I think you have your stories mixed up. There wasn't a wolf in the tale of the country mouse and—"

He waved away her explanation as he began to pace across the room. "Doesn't matter who was in which story. The moral's the same. You're in way over your head."

"Way over my head?" she repeated, clearly baffled by the conversation. "I'm not sure I know what you mean."

He whirled to face her, his face flushed with fury.

"Buzz, you blind, country mouse! He's a playboy! Gobbles up women like you every day of the week, then tosses them aside when he's done with them."

She jerked up her chin. "He was kind, a perfect gentleman and did nothing whatsoever to make me question his integrity or his intentions."

"Hah!" he cried triumphantly. "That just proves what an innocent you truly are. I saw the way he held you when y'all were dancing. The way his hands rode low on your butt. And you!" he accused, thrusting the glass in her direction again. "You were wound around him tighter than poison ivy on an oak tree."

Her mouth dropped open, then snapped closed with an angry click of teeth. "I certainly was not!"

"Yes, you were. And if I hadn't peeled you off him and hauled you back to our suite, you'd've ended up in his bed."

Her face paled, then flushed an angry red. "I most certainly would not! I haven't saved myself all these years to toss away my virginity to the first man who shows me a little attention."

She clapped a hand over her mouth, her face draining of color. Then, with a strangled sob, she threw his tuxedo jacket at him and ran for her room.

Erik caught the jacket before it struck his face, wincing at the furious slam of her door.

*A virgin? Had the mouse just confessed to being a virgin?*

He turned for the bar, the bourbon slowing his ability to absorb the full meaning of her confession. After fumbling open another bottle of bourbon, he tossed it back, not even bothering with a glass this time. Shuddering as the liquor seared his throat, he braced his hands on the bar and stared at his secretary's door.

A virgin? he asked himself again, then laughed.

Hell, he hadn't thought there was one left in the entire world.

Erik lay flat on his back, his fingers laced over his chest, staring at the hotel bedroom's ceiling. Moonlight spilled through the wide window and across his chest, a reminder that he'd forgotten to pull the drapes before crawling into bed.

A virgin, he thought again, unable to shake Penny's startling disclosure from his mind. His secretary was a virgin. He frowned, trying to recall the details of the résumé Mrs. H. had faxed to him while he was in Japan. She was in her late twenties, if he remembered correctly.

He shook his head, unable to believe that a woman could reach that age with her virginity still intact.

How? he asked himself, shifting his mind easily into an analytical mode. And why? She wasn't bad looking...or, at least, she wasn't when she got all dolled up. Surely there had to be at least one man in her past with whom she'd had a physical relationship.

He shook his head and rolled to his side, punching his pillow beneath his head. No way, he told himself. She couldn't be a virgin. Not with a body like that.

At the thought, an image pushed itself into his mind of her standing in the ballroom in that poor excuse of a dress, her breasts straining against the formed cups of stiff satin that were all that kept those delectable mounds from exploding right out the top. The way the clingy, glittery fabric hugged her body like a second skin, accentuating a slender waist and full, sensuous hips. The brush of carrot-red hair against creamy, smooth shoulders. Moist, full lips, glossed to invite a man's kiss.

He groaned and rolled from the bed and to his feet, knowing he'd never get any sleep now. Not when he knew a virgin slept in the room across from his. He swayed drunkenly a moment until the spinning room stilled. "A drink," he told himself, and staggered to the bedroom door. "Another drink and I'll be able to sleep."

He stepped into the living room and braced a hand against the wall for a moment to steady himself before pushing himself on toward the bar.

He twisted open another bottle of bourbon, lifted it to his lips, then froze, listening. Frowning, he lowered the bottle and turned to peer at Penny's closed bedroom door, sure that the muffled sound had come from behind it. Was she crying? he wondered, his gut knotting in dread.

He set aside the bottle and started for her door. He stumped his toe against a leg of the sofa, swore ripely, then limped his way across the remaining length of the room. Leaning a shoulder against her bedroom door, he pressed his ear to the wood and listened. For a moment he heard nothing but the rasp of his own labored breathing…but then distinctly heard again the muffled sound of sobbing.

His heart twisting in his chest at the mournful sound, he pushed open the door, not bothering to knock. Unlike him, his secretary had remembered to pull the drapes in her room, leaving only a strip of light leaking from beneath the bathroom door for illumination. Wondering if she'd slipped in the tub and hurt herself, he tiptoed to the closed door.

He pressed his ear against the wood, heard her soft

sobbing and reached for the doorknob, intending to
only test to see if it was locked. "Penny?" he called
uncertainly. The knob gave in his hand and the door
opened a crack. He stared at it and weighed his op-
tions, knowing full well he ought to turn right around
and head back for his room.

A virgin, he thought again, and pressed a palm
against the door, pushing it open, her innocence calling to him like a siren in the night.

She lay in the tub with her head tilted back against
its sloped end and bath bubbles nudging at her chin.
She had her arms raised above the water, her hands
pressed tightly over her face—a failed effort to hide
the sound of her crying from him, he was sure. Lighted
candles lined both sides of the marble tub, completely
surrounding her, their flickering, golden light giving
her bare skin an ethereal glow.

Unsure if it was the pitiful sound of her sobs that
drew him or the knowledge that she was naked beneath the bubbles, Erik eased closer to the tub.
"Penny?"

At the sound of his voice, she snatched her hands
from her face and twisted her head around, her tear-
drenched eyes widening in alarm when she saw him.
He took a step closer, and she slid lower beneath the
bubbles, flattening her hands over her breasts. The protective action only served to push the bubbles away,
revealing more bare skin and the pinkened bud of one
nipple peeking from between her spread fingers.

"What are you doing in here?" she cried.

His mouth dry as cotton, Erik had to swallow before
he could reply. "I...I heard you crying."

She whipped her head around to face the opposite
end of the tub, her cheeks as bright a red as the hair

she'd piled carelessly on top of her head. "I wasn't crying. I...I was singing."

"Singing?" He choked on a laugh as he picked up the two candles closest to him and relocated them farther down the side of the tub. "Hope you don't have plans of making a career of it," he said, as he seated himself on the edge of the tub.

She inched away from him, her hands still clamped over her breasts. Her tongue darted out and slicked nervously over her lips. "I...I don't."

He bit back a smile at the quaver he heard in her voice. Yeah, she was a mouse all right. She might *seem* like a different person when she got all dolled up, but stripped down she was still essentially a mouse. Bracing his hands on his thigh, he leaned across the side of the bubble-filled tub. "Good. 'Cause I'd hate to lose another secretary."

She drew back, her eyes riveted on his face. "You're drunk," she accused in a hoarse whisper.

He chuckled and shook his head. "Not enough to do what you're afraid I'm here to do."

Her eyes grew round and her lips parted, indicating her surprise that he'd managed to read her thoughts so easily.

"Then leave," she said and attempted to drill a hole in the opposite side of the tub with her shoulder.

He lifted his hands helplessly. "Can't."

"Can't?" she repeated in disbelief.

"Nope."

"And may I ask why not?" she asked, regaining a bit of the fiery temper he'd had the distinct pleasure of witnessing only a handful of times over the past two days.

"I can't sleep," he said, as if that explained everything.

"Well, you certainly won't be able to do so while sitting on the side of my tub." She hazarded exposure by lifting a hand and giving his arm an angry shove. "Go," she ordered, and sat up high enough to snatch a towel from the brass rack hanging on the wall just above her head. She quickly stood, watery bubbles sluicing down her legs as she whipped the towel around her upper body, but did only a moderate job of covering her nudity.

When he remained on the side of the tub, she lifted a hand and pointed at the door. "Go," she repeated more firmly.

With a sigh he pushed to his feet. "Okay," he said in defeat. "If you insist."

He probably would have left then, too, if he hadn't noticed that her gaze slid to his waist, then lower, locking on his black briefs. He watched her eyelids slam shut, heard the rasp of a desperately drawn breath...and he took a step closer to the tub.

"Penny?"

She flipped her eyes wide, gripping the ends of the towel tighter between her breasts. "What?"

"Would you give me a good-night kiss?" He lifted a hand, opening a space between his thumb and index finger that measured less than an inch. "Just a little one."

He watched her throat convulse in a swallow, her gaze drop to his mouth and had to struggle to keep from grinning from ear to ear. "Please?" he added, hoping to sway her.

She lifted her gaze to his, her cheeks now as rosy

as the rest of her water-warmed body. "If I do, will you promise to leave?"

He sliced a finger twice across his heart. "Scout's honor."

She eyed him doubtfully. "You were a Boy Scout?"

"For about three months."

She hesitated a second longer, then huffed a breath. "Oh, all right. One kiss. But that's all. Then you're leaving."

"Deal," he agreed, before she had time to change her mind and send him packing. He stepped closer and cupped his hands around her elbows. He felt the leap of her pulse at even that slight a contact and had to work hard not to laugh when she closed her eyes and craned her neck, shoving her puckered lips blindly in his direction.

A virgin, he told himself, then stifled a groan when the reminder placed a rock-hard ache in his groin. Knowing he had better get this over with quickly or she wouldn't remain one for long, he leaned to touch his mouth to hers. "Relax," he murmured as he brushed his lips over her tightly puckered mouth.

She jerked her head back. "Okay," she said breathlessly, slicking her lips again. "You've had your kiss. Now go."

His brows shot up. "You call that a kiss?"

"Well, yes," she replied, looking uncertain.

He dropped his head back and laughed. "That wasn't a kiss. That was an accidental meeting of mouths."

"Look," she warned. "You promised."

"I'm leaving," he assured her, then added, "Just as soon as I get my kiss."

She dropped her shoulders in frustration. "Fine." She slicked her lips again. "But this is your last chance."

He gave her elbows a tug, pulling her closer. "No problem." He watched her eyes close, but before she could pucker her lips again, he slammed his mouth against hers, taking her totally by surprise. He smiled against her lips, softening the kiss as she stared at him in cross-eyed dismay over a little button of a nose. She's cute, he realized with a suddenness that had his fingers convulsing on her elbows. More than cute. She was downright sexy.

And her taste. He groaned and slowly traced his tongue along the crease of her lips in a slow bid for admittance, hoping to savor more of her tantalizing flavor. "Yeah," he encouraged as her lips parted beneath his on a trembling sigh. "Like that." He deepened the kiss, waited a heartbeat, then slipped his tongue inside.

He felt her stiffen at the unexpected invasion…then the slow, languid melt of her body as he stroked his tongue along hers in a sensual dance. The fingers she'd held fisted tightly between her breasts fluttered open, and the towel dropped to sink beneath the mountains of iridescent bubbles. With a muffled whimper, she lifted her arms and looped them around his neck.

The ache in his groin twisted tighter when her nipples stabbed at his chest. Moaning, he drew her closer, then groaned when she began to move her tongue in a teasing rhythm with his.

A virgin? he asked himself as she rocked her body suggestively against his. Maybe she'd lied. Maybe she had more experience than she'd wanted to admit. Maybe this was all a game of some kind. A game of

seduction he had yet to encounter—though he was
sure he'd fallen prey to every form of female seduction
known to man.

Convinced by her passionate response to his kiss,
the sensuous sway of her body against his, the desperate claw of her fingers against his neck, that he was
dealing with a woman who knew her way around a
man's bedroom, he slid his hands down her back, dug
his fingers deeply into her buttocks and brought her
hips up hard against his.

He knew instantly that he'd made a mistake. As
soon as he introduced her to his erection, she went
stiff as a board in his arms and her eyes did that cross-
eyed thing again, wide and staring in what looked suspiciously to him like terror. Slowly he relaxed his grip
on her buttocks and eased his hips from hers. Slower
still he broke the all-but-welded connection of their
mouths and took a step back until their gazes met.

She gulped, then swallowed, her eyes wide and unblinking. "I...I think you'd better go now."

He took another step back and made a second mistake when he let his gaze drop to her chest. The twin
mounds, fully exposed now without the towel to cover
them and reddened from chafing against his chest, rose
and fell like bellows with each breath she drew. Surrounded by darker, rose-tinted flesh, her nipples stood
at rapt attention, seeming to beg for his touch and his
mouth.

Though he'd been close to certifiably drunk when
he'd entered the room, he suddenly found himself
stone-cold sober. Fearing if he didn't leave, he'd do
something really stupid, something he was sure he
would regret by morning, he backed toward the door.

"Yeah. I guess I'd better."

# Four

Once Erik reached his own room, though, and crawled into his bed, he had second thoughts about his decision to leave.

Damn, but she was something, he thought as he punched his pillow up beneath his head. Imagine a woman hiding all those sumptuous curves beneath a shapeless business suit. He shook his head in regret. What a waste.

And her response to him! He'd been with a lot of women, but he didn't remember ever running across one who could send his blood pressure shooting through the top of his head with a simple stroke of her tongue.

Feeling the uncomfortable swell of his sex, he lifted his head to peer at the door. Maybe if he—

He dropped his head back to his pillow. No way. If he went back to her room, she'd probably scream sexual harassment. It wasn't as if she'd invited him into her bathroom. He'd barged in and, once there, refused to budge when she'd asked him to leave.

A smile spread across his face as he envisioned her standing in the tub, bubbles sluicing down over her curves...and wondered what old Buzz would say if he learned that Erik had gotten a sneak preview of Penny's feminine charms.

Frowning at the thought of his friend, he pushed himself up to his elbows, remembering how Penny had raved on and on about what a gentleman Buzz was, what a skillful dancer he had proved to be. Hell, to hear her talk, the guy could all but walk on water!

He flopped to his back and folded his arms across his chest, scowling at the ceiling. Well, Erik Thompson was more a gentleman than Buzz Kenney could ever hope to be, he told himself. The opportunity to demonstrate his finer points to Penny just hadn't presented itself yet.

There wasn't a man alive who could romance a woman with more finesse than Erik Thompson. Nor was there one who knew how to please a woman more once he got her into his bed.

And he'd get Penny there, he promised himself. And it would be her idea, not his. Or at least she'd think it was hers. All he had to do was show her a few of his finer points, prove to her what a gentleman he could be, pour on a little of that Cyber Cowboy charm.

And he'd do just that, he told himself with a confident smile as he closed his eyes. Starting first thing in the morning.

The next morning Penny postponed leaving her room as long as she dared, dreading facing her em-

ployer after the humiliations she'd suffered the night
before.

"A virgin," she moaned miserably, remembering.
What had possessed her to foolishly confess her innocence to a man as worldly and experienced as Erik
Thompson? And why had she insisted he leave when
for years she'd wanted so desperately for him to be
the one to free her of that stigma?

Knowing she couldn't hide in her room all day, she
moved to stand before the dresser mirror, checking her
appearance one last time before facing him again. She
smoothed her hands down the front of the yellow, calf-
length sundress she'd purchased the afternoon before,
studying her reflection with a critical eye. Though not
nearly as jazzy as the dress she'd worn the previous
evening, the sundress was stylish yet simple and promised to be a functional addition to the new wardrobe
she intended to build. The earrings, though, might be
a bit much, she thought uneasily as she touched a finger to the large gold-and-bronze leaf dangling from
her earlobe.

Don't be silly, she told herself and turned from the
mirror. She often saw women wearing much flashier
jewelry than the hammered-metal earrings the clerk
had insisted would look perfect with the dress. It was
simply her nerves that were making her question the
selection now.

Reminded of the cause of her nervousness, she
glanced uneasily at the closed door, then squared her
shoulders and drew in a deep breath. Pretend it never
happened, she told herself. Simply blot the embarrassing incident from your mind. More than likely a man
with Erik's reputation with women wouldn't have

given another thought to seeing a woman as unappealing as Penny Rawley standing naked in a tub, dripping bath bubbles.

With that reassuring thought, she opened the door and stepped into the suite's living room.

At her entrance Erik turned from the open balcony doors. "Good morning."

Every assurance she'd given herself that he wouldn't remember the previous night's events slipped away when confronted with his knowing smile, leaving her feeling weak, exposed and pitifully vulnerable. "G-good morning, Mr. Thompson."

He clucked his tongue in disapproval. "Erik. Please."

Surprised by his request for informality, she slowly nodded her head. "All right...Erik."

Seemingly satisfied, he smiled again and opened an arm wide in invitation toward the balcony. "I ordered breakfast for us. I hope you don't mind."

She glanced past him to the balcony and the linen-draped table arranged for an intimate breakfast for two. Swallowing hard, she forced her gaze from the silver-domed platters and the slender column of crystal holding a single yellow rose and back to him. "No. I don't mind."

"Excellent. Then why don't we eat before our food grows cold?"

She hesitated a moment longer, not sure she should trust him. The dramatic change in his behavior was enough to make anyone question his motives. His warm and charming demeanor was a startling contrast to his usual scowling indifference and his equally irritating domineering attitude toward her. And the sultry smile he continued to grace her with... Well, it

gave her a better understanding why women all but
fell at his feet to gain his attention, and why *People
Weekly* magazine had ranked him in their top-ten list
of the world's most eligible bachelors.

Fearing he would hear her knees knocking together
if she hesitated much longer, she forced herself to
cross the room and step out onto the balcony. She
jumped, startled, when he reached around her and
pulled out a chair. But when he merely inclined his
head and dipped a hand in invitation, she sank weakly
down onto the chair he held for her.

After seating himself opposite her, he lifted one of
the domed lids, closed his eyes and inhaled deeply.
"Eggs Benedict," he said almost reverently, then
opened his eyes to meet her gaze. "Do you like
them?"

"Y-yes," she stammered, unable to tear her gaze
from the unfamiliar warmth in his bedroom-blue eyes.

"I'd hoped you would." He served her, then himself. After slicing a neat wedge from the gourmet dish,
he slipped it between his lips, then closed his eyes
again and moaned deep in his throat. "Delicious," he
murmured, then opened his eyes and waved his fork
at her plate. "Eat. I've got a full schedule planned for
us today."

Though it took all her strength to do so, Penny obediently lifted her fork and turned her attention to her
meal. "Do we have meetings?"

He smiled as he filled a tall, slender flute with a
decadent blend of orange juice and champagne. He
offered it to her across the table. "No…at least not of
a business nature."

Swallowing hard, she accepted the glass. "What
then?"

He winked and lifted his glass in a silent toast. "You'll see soon enough."

Penny couldn't remember the last time she'd visited a zoo. Long before her parents' deaths, that was for sure. But she'd *never* ridden in a convertible sports car driven by a breathtakingly handsome man, with the wind whipping mercilessly through her hair. Nor had she had her face dampened by a fine mist of ocean spray while sailing across the sparkling surface of a sun-kissed bay, her hand linked with that of a sexy multimillionaire. And she'd never had dinner before a campfire on a beach with a man stretched out at her side, while the tide tugged the edge of the water farther and farther away from her bare feet. But more, she had never experienced with a man the slow build of intimacy that she'd sensed developing between her and Erik during the day they'd spent together.

Even as she reflected on these firsts, he caught her hand and laced his fingers through hers. "What are you thinking?"

A shiver chased down her spine as she looked down at him, unable to think of anything but the strength and power hidden in the fingers linked with hers, the intimacy his husky voice suggested, the warmth in his blue eyes. Though tempted to reply with a vague "nothing" and avoid giving him the proof he needed to support his claim that she was indeed the country mouse in the city he'd pronounced her to be…she discovered she could only offer him the truth. "About all the firsts I've experienced today."

His gaze on hers, he drew her hand to his lips and pressed a kiss against her knuckles, sending shivers chasing down her spine.

"There are a few more firsts I'd like to introduce you to."

Her eyes snapped to a sharp focus and she stiffened, wondering if losing her virginity was one of the other firsts to which he referred.

He pushed himself to his feet, drawing her to her feet, as well. "Ever walked barefoot on a moonlit beach?"

"Uh...no," she stammered, embarrassed that she'd thought he was referring to sex, when he'd only meant something as innocent as a stroll along the beach.

He drew her to his side and led her to the edge of the ocean. She gasped when the cold water lapped over her bare toes. He laughed at her reaction and dropped down to hunker at her feet. She felt his fingers brush over her ankle, then curve around her calf, and she curled her toes into the sand as heat rose to churn in her belly.

"What are you doing?" she asked, finding it difficult to breathe as she watched him unfasten the lower buttons of her sundress' skirt.

"Tying up the hem of your dress." He looked up at her and reassured her with a wink. "Wouldn't want you to get it wet."

She shivered as his knuckles chafed against the skin he'd exposed, then waited nervously while he rolled his pant legs up to just below his knees. Oddly, she found the dark hair that shadowed his muscled calves unbelievably sexy.

Taking her hand again, he drew her along with him, wrapping an arm loosely around her waist as he started down the beach. They walked a ways in comfortable silence, their hips bumping occasionally. Penny couldn't remember a single event in her past that equaled the pleasure of simply strolling along at his side, or one that topped the magical mood created by the moonlit night.

"Have you had a good time today?"

"Oh, yes," she assured him. "Very."

He stopped and turned her into the circle of his arms. "Good. I'd hoped you would."

Her pulse leaped at the warmth she saw in his eyes. She knew he was going to kiss her, could see his intent in the darkening of his eyes, could feel it in the increased tension in the arms he'd looped around her waist. She dropped her gaze to his lips and wet her own, impatient for the feel of his mouth on hers again.

Though their kiss the night before had lacked the romantic embellishments of the moonlit beach, she remembered every detail as if it had been etched upon her very soul. The commanding pressure of his mouth. The sharp flavor of bourbon she'd tasted when he'd slipped his tongue between her lips. Wave after wave of sensation that had rolled through her body when he'd first touched his tongue to hers, the gripping pleasure when he'd mated with it. The strength in the chest that had pushed urgently against her breasts.

The weakness.

The need.

With her gaze on his, she rose to the balls of her feet and touched her lips to his. Satin, she thought with a sigh. His lips were like firm, plump pillows of moist satin giving beneath hers. The taste of bourbon was missing this time, but the flavors she found in its place were just as heady, leaving her feeling as light-headed as if she had enjoyed one too many glasses of wine.

Wanting more of him, needing more, she looped her arms around his neck and drew his face closer to hers.

Curious—and amazingly confident—she slipped her tongue between his lips and swept it across the front of his teeth. The groan that rumbled low in his chest and crawled up his throat to vibrate against her mouth made her shiver, and she withdrew to sink back to her bare feet. Weak, she dropped her forehead against his chin. "Wow," she said, releasing a shuddery breath, then lifted her face to look up at him. "Wow," she whispered, the heat in his eyes adding a new depth to the warmth that already pulsed in her cheeks and swirled in her belly.

He slid his hands down her back to cup her buttocks. "Yeah," he agreed, his voice husky. "Wow."

He drew her hips against his, but kept his gaze on hers, as if monitoring her reaction. Remembering the shock she'd felt the night before upon encountering the unexpected hardness of his arousal, she waited, too, anticipating the same fear to grip her now. But when his hips met hers and the column of firm flesh pressed against her abdomen, there was no shock, no fear, no hesitancy. Just a burning need to feel more of him. To have him inside her.

He must have sensed the change in her response, because the tension eased from his face and arms, and his eyes grew darker, sharper. With his hands gripped firmly around her buttocks, holding her against him, he lowered his head and opened his mouth over hers, his possession of her instant and complete. He drank deeply, yet with a gentleness that drew tears to her eyes.

He spun the kiss out, each stroke of his tongue leaving her hotter, weaker. Then, when she was sure she'd die if he didn't take her, he relaxed the hands he gripped at her buttocks and smoothed his palms slowly up her back, forcing her more firmly against his chest, until her aching breasts were flattened between them.

She whimpered her frustration, her desire for him, and he tightened his arms around her as he lifted her high on his chest, swallowing the sound. Holding her against him, he turned in a slow, mind-dizzying circle, never once moving his lips from hers.

Weakened by the devastating power of his kiss, yet throbbing with a need that rivaled the pounding crash of the waves over the rocks just beyond them, she drew her hands to his face. She thrilled at the high ridge of cheekbone beneath her palms, the scrape of a day's growth of beard against her fingers as she drew her hands along his jaw, the hard cords of muscle she discovered when she dropped them to his shoulders and clung.

Groaning, he sank to his knees on the sand, then to his back, drawing her over him. He plunged his tongue deeply into her mouth. An ache spread through her chest, mirroring in intensity the one that throbbed low in her belly. And when he caught her face between his hands and tore his mouth from hers, she didn't even try to suppress the moan of frustration the loss drew.

"I want you."

Slowly she forced her eyes open and found the want he'd stated flaming in his eyes. He increased the pressure of his hands, and she could feel the tension in them, a need surely as strong as hers for him.

"I want you," he said again, then frowned. "But not here."

She knew he was right. The beach was too open, too public. The chance of someone happening upon them too great. But knowing that didn't stop the dis-

appointment that rushed through her. Nor did it ease
the ache that twisted inside her.

Fitting his hands at her waist, he shifted her off him,
then pushed himself to his feet and grabbed her hand,
pulling her to her feet, as well. He caught her by the
waist again and hauled her to him for one last hungry
kiss, before tucking her against his side and walking
with her back to their blanket and the campfire that
had burned low in their absence.

They made the drive back to the hotel in silence,
each painfully aware of the other's nearness, of what
awaited them once they arrived. In the hotel's glass
elevator that carried them to the uppermost floor, they
stood side by side, both with their gazes locked on the
digital monitor that registered their frustratingly slow
ascent. They didn't dare to so much as glance at the
other, or touch, for fear what would happen if they
did.

But when the elevator stopped and they finally
stepped inside their hotel suite and closed the door
behind them, offering them the privacy that the beach
hadn't, they fell into each other's arms. Their mouths
were urgent, demanding, greedy, their hands clawing
and desperate as they came together, as if time and
circumstances had never separated them at all.

Articles of clothing flew across the room as they
stripped each other of the frustrating barriers that separated them. But when they were naked and standing
less than a foot apart, they could only stare, their gazes
locked, their chests heaving as if they'd run from the
beach to the hotel, rather than driven there.

Erik was the first to move, the first to break the
silence. Inhaling deeply, he lifted a hand and placed
it over her quivering breast. ''Beautiful,'' he said, and

dropped his gaze to stare. "So, so beautiful," he murmured, and dipped his head to stroke his tongue across the budded nipple he drew between finger and thumb.

Penny gasped, arching against him as he opened his mouth fully over her breast. And when he slowly drew her in, she knotted her fingers in his hair and clamped her teeth together, willing herself to remain upright.

Hot arrows of need shot to her center as he suckled, leaving her moist, aching…wanting. But before she could voice her need for him, beg him to make love to her, to end this slow torture, he had shifted again and was thrusting his tongue deeply into her mouth, stealing her breath.

"My room," he said breathlessly as he rained kisses over her face and down her neck. Without waiting for her response, he scooped her up into his arms and headed there.

The impatient beep of an electronic alarm had him skidding to a stop halfway across the living room.

He whipped his head around to stare at the laptop computer he'd left on the bar. With a low, furious growl, he dumped Penny over the back of the sofa and raced for it. Positioning his fingers over the keyboard, he viciously keyed in instructions.

"Come on," he growled, his gaze riveted on the screen as he watched rows of numbers jump into view with a slowness that had him swearing.

Across the room Penny slowly pulled herself to a sitting position on the sofa, staring at his bare backside, her eyes wide in disbelief. Had he really just tossed her aside as carelessly as a child would a toy he'd grown bored with? Could he possibly think that something, *anything* was more important than what was happening between them, what was about to happen between them when the alarm had sounded?

She eased to the edge of the sofa, then slowly to her feet, her legs trembling uncontrollably, her gaze riveted on his back. How could he? she asked herself as hot, angry tears filled her eyes. Did he think so little of her, of what she was offering him, that he would choose a stupid computer over *her*?

Realizing the answer to her question stood right before her without a stitch of clothing on, pounding a keyboard like a maniac, she hiccuped a sob and turned and fled to her room, slamming and locking the door behind her.

While Penny was making her tearful exit, Erik was punching keys and watching the screen, monitoring Boy Wonder's progress into the secure system the hacker had breached.

"What are you doing, kid?" he muttered, narrowing his eyes on the screen. "What is it you want?"

With thousands of miles separating him from the attacker, Erik could only watch as the usurper slipped into the back door of Erik's own company, Cyber Cowboy International, and blatantly crawled his way through protected files. Slamming a fist against the bar's marble surface and swearing, he positioned his fingers over the keyboard again and angrily punched in codes, slamming doors behind the unknown hacker.

As quickly as he had appeared, Boy Wonder disappeared, leaving Erik staring at nothing but a silent, blinking cursor.

He spun, raking his fingers through his hair, to pace to the balcony doors and back. "Damn that miserable hacker. That's the last time that bastard will thumb his nose at me."

He stopped and turned, suddenly remembering Penny. When he didn't see her on the sofa where he'd left her, he strode to her door, thinking she'd gone into her bedroom. He twisted the knob and frowned when he found it locked. "Penny?"

He waited, listening, then lifted a hand and pounded a fist on the door. "Hey, Penny! Open up!"

"Go away."

His frown deepened when he heard the tears in her voice. He muttered a curse, realizing too late that he'd probably offended her by dumping her on the sofa when he'd responded to the alarm. Frustrated, yet hopeful that he could persuade her to open the door and they could pick up where they had left off, he placed a fist against the door and pressed his forehead against it. "Come on, honey," he pleaded. "I'm sorry. It was that damn hacker again. You know. Boy Wonder. The one who's been breaking into my system."

"Go away," she said more loudly this time, her voice sharp with resentment, "and play with your stupid toys."

He dropped his hand from the door and curled his fingers into a tighter fist. "Computers aren't toys," he shouted. "They're highly technical, electronic equipment."

"Fine. Then go play with your highly technical, electronic *toys*."

Setting his jaw against the fury that raged inside him, he backed from the door. "All right, dammit!" he yelled. "If that's the way you want it. Fine. But pack your bags. We're going back to Texas."

Wheeling sharply, he stormed across the room, snatched his laptop from the bar, ripped the modem connection from the phone jack and stomped to his room, slamming the door behind him.

Penny slept throughout the late-night flight back to Austin. Her ability to sleep in the face of so much turmoil and after such an exhausting display of emotion didn't surprise her. She often crawled into bed, pulled the covers over her head and slept when confronted with seemingly insurmountable problems or fears. She supposed the technique was a form of avoidance, much like the ostrich who buried his head in the sand when sensing danger, but she didn't care. She'd discovered the strategy quite by accident following the death of her parents and had perfected the technique over the years. On this particular night it served her well.

And frustrated the hell out of Erik.

He didn't want Penny to sleep. He wanted her in his lap, in his arms, kissing him and clawing at him as she had earlier that evening. Instead, once they'd settled into his private jet for the flight back to Texas, she'd pulled a blanket over her shoulder, turned her back on him and closed her eyes. She'd slept ever since, successfully shutting him out.

Well, that was just fine, he told himself, and rammed his seat back to a reclining position. Two could play this game as well as one.

Unfortunately he discovered he didn't share the mouse's ability to sleep in the face of turmoil. His mind refused to let go of the memories he'd unknowingly stored away of the day they'd spent together exploring San Diego.

In spite of his determination to block them, images and scenes scrolled through his mind with a clarity that rivaled a DVD movie. Her childish delight in watching the koala bears play at the San Diego Zoo. The way her eyes had sparkled with laughter and her lips had gleamed as she'd nibbled her way around a roasted ear of buttery corn on the cob he'd purchased for her from a vendor on the beach. The way the wind had whipped through her hair, much as it had the colorful flags that topped the mast of the sailboat he'd chartered for their afternoon sail around Mission Bay.

But the most stubborn images, the ones that returned again and again, keeping him awake, were those at the beach and those, later, at the hotel. The soft, dreamy expression on her face as she'd watched the ocean waves rush onto shore. The wonder in her eyes when she'd tipped her head back to stare at the canopy of winking stars overhead. The breathless expectancy with which she'd looked up at him when he'd turned her into his arms. The feel of her hands on his flesh, the silky texture of hers beneath his. The heat that had pulsed and throbbed between them when he'd held her in his arms. The scent of her that still filled his senses, the sensuous curves that had once filled his hands.

When he'd set out that morning, his goal had been to get her into his bed, to claim the ultimate prize of her virginity.

But that was before he'd watched her face light up with laughter as she'd watched the koala bears at the zoo. Before he had kissed her. Before he had held her in his arms. Before he had tasted her innocence, experienced his own knee-jerk reaction to her passionate response.

Now he'd be satisfied if she'd just look at him, talk to him…quit ignoring him.

And if she were to touch him, he thought, dragging a shaky hand down his face. He'd be putty in her hands.

# Five

Penny gave a great deal of thought to simply resigning from her job and finding a new one, thus putting an end to the torture of having to see Erik every day— a plan her friend Suzy, after hearing the details of what all had transpired in California, had loudly applauded.

And, coward that she was, the old Penny probably would have resigned. But the new Penny, the one who had first made an appearance when Penny had made the decision to leave her brother's home, the one who had grown stronger and more confident as she'd tackled the daunting task of settling into a new apartment, a new job and a new town. The new Penny who had seemingly blossomed overnight, the new Penny with the fabulous new hairstyle, the one who had spent a small fortune at a specialty shop with the intent of building a new wardrobe that reflected her rebirth and her bold step toward an exciting new future. The

Penny who had stood up to Erik, defied his anger, his
fury, in order to protect her heart.... That Penny
wouldn't quit. To do so would be admitting her cow-
ardice, knuckling under to her fears, returning to her
old ways, her old self.

And the new Penny had no intention of ever returning there.

But dealing with Erik, hiding from him her disappointment, her resentment at having been so carelessly
treated, would take finesse and a strength she only
prayed she possessed.

A week after her return from the business trip to
California with Erik, Penny glanced up from her computer screen as the elevator doors slid open.

"Mrs. Hilloughby!" she cried, rising as the former
secretary stepped from the elevator. She circled her
desk to greet the woman, offering her hands in greeting. "How nice to see you again. How are you?"

Eleanor Hilloughby grabbed Penny's hands and
squeezed. "Just the same. But you!" she exclaimed,
drawing back to give Penny a thorough inspection.
"What have you done to yourself?"

Penny lowered her gaze, blushing. "I cut my hair."

Eleanor nodded her approval. "And it suits you.
Gives you a whole new look."

Penny smiled, pleased with the woman's assessment. "Thank you. But what are you doing here? I
would think you'd be off playing with your grandchildren."

Eleanor blew a breath up at the wisps of salt-and-
pepper hair that fell across her forehead. "I'm taking
the day off. I don't know where those children get all
that energy. Totally wear me out in no time flat."

Penny laughed and drew the woman into the reception area. "Would you like a cup of coffee? Or perhaps some iced tea?"

"Tea, please." Eleanor watched as Penny went about filling glasses. Though she was dying to know how her replacement and Erik were getting along, Eleanor wouldn't allow herself to simply ask outright, for fear of embarrassing the young woman. But there were other ways to obtain the information she needed, she thought slyly. After thirty-five years as a special agent's wife, she'd picked up a trick or two she could use.

"Is Erik in his office?"

Penny's fingers fumbled on the sugar spoon's handle, spilling white granules across the serving bar. Eleanor noted the display of nerves and filed it away for later consideration.

Penny neatly dealt with the spill and at the same time avoided Eleanor's gaze. "Yes. Would you like me to tell him that you're here?"

Eleanor waved away the offer. "Time enough for that later. Tell me about you. Are you enjoying working with Erik?"

Penny's hesitation was another fact that Eleanor tucked away for later consideration.

"Yes," she finally said, and forced a smile. "I'm enjoying my work very much."

*Hmm,* Eleanor mused silently as she accepted the glass of iced tea Penny offered her. *The girl can dance her way around a question she doesn't want to answer better than a politician.*

Hoping to seek out the cause of what she feared was a tense relationship, Eleanor led the way to a cozy grouping of chairs. She sat down, then patted the cushion on the chair next to hers. "Sit and visit with me a spell."

Penny glanced uneasily at Erik's closed office door.

"Oh, for heaven's sake," Eleanor fussed. "He won't begrudge you a minute or two away from your desk."

With a last, hesitant glance at the door, Penny sank onto the chair, perching on its edge and holding her glass of iced tea between her hands, looking as if she would bolt at the slightest provocation.

Hoping to put the girl at ease, Eleanor glanced around the office and sighed. "My, but I miss this place."

Penny peered at her in surprise. "Really?"

Eleanor chuckled at the doubt she heard in her replacement's voice. "Yes, really. There's a lot to be said for retirement. But there's something to be said, too, for knowing you have somewhere to go everyday, somewhere you're needed."

Concern creased Penny's brow. "If you'd like your old job back," she began uneasily.

Eleanor laughed, quickly dismissing the suggestion with a wave of her hand. "Lord no, girl. I knew what I was doing when I retired. I have no regrets. Though I do miss seeing my Erik."

Penny lowered her gaze and dragged a finger around the top of her glass. Eleanor noted that action, as well, and suspected the cause for it was her mention of Erik. She leaned back and studied the young woman beside her, sure that something was going on between her old boss and his new secretary. And she feared that "something" wasn't what she'd hoped for when she'd hired Penny to take her place.

"He's a good man," she said, watching for Penny's

reaction. "A little too obsessed with his work, but his heart is basically in the right place."

"I'm sure you're right."

"Doesn't look after himself, though," Eleanor added, wagging her head with regret. "Forgets to eat, unless reminded."

"Yes, I've noticed that."

"But he's got a pretty face." Chuckling, Eleanor poked an elbow against Penny's arm. "You can forgive a man a lot when he's easy to look at."

Penny rose from her chair. "Looks aren't everything."

"No," Eleanor agreed, rising, as well. "But it's usually what first attracts a man or a woman to a member of the opposite sex."

"It's what's inside a person that's important," Penny insisted as she crossed to her desk.

"Yes," Eleanor replied, following her. "And, as I said, Erik's got a good heart."

Penny glanced over her shoulder, and Eleanor saw the doubt that shadowed the girl's eyes...and maybe a little hurt, as well. "Has he told you about his family?" she asked, deciding a little interference wouldn't hurt.

Penny's brow creased in a thoughtful frown as she set her glass on a coaster on her desk and settled herself in her chair. "No. He's never mentioned them."

"Didn't expect he would." Eleanor sighed heavily. "He hasn't had contact with them in years. They're a cold-hearted lot. He's their only child, yet they are so busy with their careers and lives, they never bother to spend time with him. Not even when he was young. Hired nannies and housekeepers to see to his raising." She clucked her tongue in disapproval. "Children need their families, the assurance of their love, in order to learn how to give it themselves.''

Penny stared blindly at her desktop, thinking of her brother, her nieces and nephew and knowing what Mrs. Hilloughby said was true. Hadn't she left her childhood home, her family and all that was familiar for that very reason? Hadn't she known that if she'd stayed her brother would continue to ignore his children and leave their care up to her?

And to discover that Erik might have suffered similarly, yearning for his parents' love and attention, just as her nieces and nephew had yearned for their father's, made her heart ache. Feeling the sympathy building for Erik, she quickly stiffened her spine. ''Yes, they do,'' she agreed. ''But there are plenty of people who have survived tragic childhoods and dysfunctional families and gone on to lead normal and productive lives.''

Eleanor watched Penny, hearing the pain in the girl's reply and wondering what Erik had done to cause it. And he *was* responsible for hurting Penny, she was sure. ''Yes,'' she replied thoughtfully. ''You're probably right. But I can't help but believe that there was someone in those people's lives who took the time to nurture them. Someone who stubbornly continued to offer love, suffering their own disappointments, I'm sure, when none was offered in return.''

Having shared all she dared on the subject, Eleanor tossed up her hands. ''Heavens! Would you listen to me? Trying to solve the world's problems, when I'm sure you've got pressing work to do.''

''Yes, I do, but it's always a pleasure to visit with

you.'' Penny reached for her phone. ''I'll buzz Erik and let him know you're here.''

Eleanor placed a hand over Penny's, preventing her from making the call. ''I'd rather surprise him.'' She winked as she headed for Erik's office door. ''Maybe I can even talk him into buying me lunch.''

Erik was exhausted, mentally drained, all but limp from the verbal battering Mrs. H. had delivered over the lunch she'd insisted he treat her to. And it hadn't ended with the payment of the tab. She'd trailed him back to his office building and ridden with him to the top floor and the space he'd carved out of the building for his private residence, claiming she wanted to see what he'd done with the place.

He'd known before she'd stepped across the threshold that he was in for another browbeating. Though he'd promised her repeatedly that he would hire a professional to decorate his apartment, he'd never gotten around to making the arrangements. As a result the walls were bare, the rooms echoing and empty but for the most basic of living requirements—a recliner, a wide-screen TV, a state-of-the-art stereo system and a king-size bed, which, unfortunately, he hadn't bothered to make up in the week since his return from California.

Nor had he bothered to dispose of the cartons of take-out food he'd ordered in for his meals during that week. They littered his kitchen's long, center island, completely concealing the granite surface beneath and filling the room with the foul odor of spoiled leftovers.

He'd promised his former secretary again that he would take care of outfitting his apartment, that he'd hire a decorator to make the place presentable. But

Mrs. H. had simply arched a brow, pointed to the phone and told him that he didn't need a decorator. Not when he had a more than capable secretary one floor below who could handle the details of turning this dump into a home.

And she'd stubbornly stood her ground, refusing to leave, until he'd picked up the phone and called his secretary, requesting that she come upstairs. It had galled him to make the call, to ask Penny to do anything for him, especially something as personal as decorate his apartment. Not after she'd given him the cold shoulder for more than a week. But he knew Eleanor Hilloughby well enough to know that if he hadn't made the call, she'd have simply picked up the phone and made it herself. The woman was just that bullheaded.

And though it shamed him to admit that he had knuckled under to Mrs. H.'s pressure, he soothed his ego by reminding himself of a piece of advice that Red had offered him years before, gleaned, Erik was sure, from having lived with Mrs. H. for over thirty-five years: *Better just go along with whatever she says, boy. It'll save you the bruises you'll get, beating your head against that thick skull of hers, plus the time wasted arguing. She's gonna get her way eventually. She always does.*

Chuckling at the memory, Erik opened a plastic garbage sack and tossed the empty take-out cartons inside. No sense letting Penny see that he lived like a pig, he told himself as he twisted a plastic tie around the top of the bag, securing the garbage inside. A man did have his pride, after all.

At the sound of the elevator's arrival, he stuffed the

bag into the pantry and closed the door, then headed
for the front room, already dreading the confrontation.

He and the mouse had done a good job of ignoring
each other since their return from California, each
working equally hard at the task. They spoke only
when necessary, rarely letting their eyes meet, and
both had become pretty darn good contortionists, in
order to avoid coming within touching distance of the
other.

And the entire situation was beginning to get on his
nerves, leaving him grouchier than usual and spoiling
for a fight.

He found just the incentive he needed to put him
over the ropes and into the boxing ring when the elevator doors opened and Penny stepped out.

She had a steno pad hugged against her breasts and
her chin lifted in that don't-you-dare-come-an-inch-
closer warning he'd grown to resent over the last
week.

"You wanted to see me?" she asked, refusing to
take a step farther into the room than was required to
allow the elevator doors to close behind her.

Irritated by her businesslike tone and a stance that
all but screamed *attitude,* he braced his hands on his
hips and turned his back to her to frown at the bank
of windows that stretched from floor to ceiling, revealing a panoramic view of downtown Austin.
"Eleanor wants you to decorate my apartment."

"Decorate your apartment?" she repeated in surprise.

"She says you can handle the job. Though, I have
my doubts," he added under his breath.

Having heard his less-than-flattering remark—and
having made a cursory inspection of the nearly empty

room as the elevator doors had opened—Penny replied tersely, "I assure you that anything I might suggest would be a stark improvement over your own pathetic attempts at interior design."

He shot her a scowl, then turned to face the windows again. "Nice try at insult, but I haven't attempted anything. The place looks the same as it did the day I moved in."

"That's rather obvious," she replied drolly. Then, unable to resist a closer inspection of the loft, she stepped farther into the room. She walked slowly around its perimeter, noting the placement of windows, the fireplace, the height of the ceiling, ideas already leaping to mind. "Do you have a particular style in mind? A theme?"

"Theme?"

"Yes, theme. You know," she said with an impatient wave of her hand, her attention captured for the moment by the stained and scored concrete floor. She could already see oriental rugs scattered across them. "Animal. Tropical. Brothel. You know. Theme."

"Brothel?"

Horrified that she'd let that particular suggestion slip—the decor she'd envisioned each time she thought of Erik's private apartment above their offices and the women he must surely entertain there—she squinted her eyes, pretending interest in the details of the architectural moldings surrounding the windows. "Poor choice of words," she said, while frantically trying to think of another. "Bachelor pad. Yes," she said, and turned, relieved that she'd thought of an alternative so quickly. "Bachelor pad is probably a much more accurate term."

He eyed her doubtfully. "Are you sure you can handle this job?"

"Of course I can," she insisted, praying he didn't take back the offer, not after she'd seen his loft apartment and all the possibilities it offered.

Frowning, he pulled a wallet from the back pocket of his jeans and pulled out a card. He tossed the piece of plastic at her.

She caught it, noting the American Express emblem and its platinum status, then looked up at him questioningly.

He waved a hand at the card. "Buy what you need and charge it to me." He turned for the open doorway that led to the kitchen. "I'm leaving town. Gone for two weeks. Have it done before I get back."

Stunned, she stared after him. "But you haven't stated your preferences!" she cried and ran after him. "What colors you favor. What style of furniture you like best. What theme!"

In the kitchen he stopped and snatched a glass from the cupboard. "Do whatever you want to the place. Just have it done by the time I get back."

Exhausted, Penny brushed back a lock of hair that had escaped the bandanna she'd tied around her hair as she stepped back to study the sage-green color she was painting the living room walls of Erik's apartment.

Her deadline was almost up. Nearly two weeks had passed since he had instructed her to decorate his loft apartment. Two weeks in which she'd spent every available minute when not at her desk at the office, shopping for and ordering furniture, studying fabric samples and paint chips and praying all the while that Erik would approve of the selections she'd made.

Not that she particularly cared whether he was pleased with *her,* she thought with a sniff of resentment. She just didn't want him to find fault with her abilities or her taste.

Glancing at her wristwatch, she bit back a groan when she saw that it was already after two in the morning. She dragged her arm across her forehead, streaking her already paint-splattered face with more of the sage-green color. If she wasn't so determined to complete the task before Erik's expected return on Monday, she would be at home in bed by now and asleep.

She sighed again and picked up the paint tray and roller, sidestepping the ladder she'd placed in the middle of the room as she headed for the kitchen to clean her equipment. With each step she silently bemoaned her stubbornness—a Rawley trait she hadn't known she possessed until now, but a family trait she'd witnessed often enough in her brother, Jase, to recognize it when it reared its ugly head.

At the thought of her brother, she smiled wistfully, missing her family and wondering how they were managing with the nanny and housekeeper she'd hired as her replacement. Though tempted a hundred times or more since leaving the ranch to call and check on them, she had resisted the temptation, fearing that if she did call, Jase would manage to coerce her into returning to the ranch and working for him again. Her brother had a gift at using guilt to maneuver Penny into toeing the line he'd drawn for her since becoming appointed her guardian and accepting responsibility for her care.

With her arms elbow deep in sudsy water, she paused in cleaning her paint tools and lifted her head, staring out the dark window above the kitchen sink, her thoughts of her brother and her past bringing to mind Mrs. Hilloughby's comment about Erik's childhood: *They're a cold-hearted lot. He's their only child, yet they are so busy with their careers and lives, they never bother to spend time with him. Not even when he was a young. Hired nannies and housekeepers to see to his raising.*

Penny didn't want to feel anything for Erik Thompson, not after he'd treated her so callously, so thoughtlessly, yet she couldn't suppress the swell of sympathy that rose for the lonely little boy he once must have been. She had known loneliness after her parents' deaths, had experienced a bone-deep longing for love and affection that her brother had never been able to adequately provide and couldn't help wondering if Erik had suffered similarly.

Tears filled her eyes, blurring the lights that shaped Austin's night skyline, as she realized that Erik must surely have suffered the same loneliness, the same need for affection that she'd experienced as a young girl. Perhaps even more so. At least she'd had her brother.

*Children need their families, the assurance of their love, in order to learn how to give it themselves.*

Mrs. Hilloughby's words pushed themselves into her mind, stirring even more troublesome questions.

Was Erik's callousness and thoughtlessness a product of the loveless home he'd grown up in, an only child all but ignored by his parents? Had he given Penny carte blanche in decorating his home because a home meant nothing to him, other than a place to sleep, a base from which to work? Was that why he'd chosen to reserve the uppermost floor of the building he'd purchased for his growing company, instead of purchasing a luxurious home in the hills of Austin or perhaps in one of the prestigious gated communities on Lake Travis, as so many other high-tech executives had done?

A shiver chased down her spine as she was forced to acknowledge that all her silent assumptions were probably correct. Erik had never had a family member to look after him or care for him as she'd had. He'd never experienced a parent's warmth and love, nor the comfort and reassurance of a home built on that strong foundation. He had chosen the location of his residence for its proximity to the one thing he *did* know and understand.

His business.

Blinking back tears, Penny finished cleaning the paint tray and roller, then set them out to dry on newspapers she'd spread to protect the granite countertops in the kitchen.

As she headed for Erik's bedroom, she was well aware that her reasons for creating a warm and comfortable environment for her employer had been self-serving in the beginning, an opportunity to prove to him that she could handle any job he tossed her way. But now they had taken on a new purpose.

She wanted to create for him the home he'd never had.

She stopped in the doorway to his bedroom, studying with a more critical eye the one room she'd managed to completely decorate: the warm, paprika-colored walls she'd painted, softened further by lamplight; the king-size bed with the cushy down

PEGGY MORELAND                                        89

comforter and the mountains of inviting pillows she'd
plumped at its head; the oversize armoire that held his
wide-screen TV, state-of-the-art entertainment center
and sound system. The bedside table she'd snugged
close to the bed, on which she'd neatly arranged the
books and reports she'd found scattered on the floor
beside the unmade bed she'd encountered upon entering his bedroom for the first time. The alarm clock
she'd positioned close at hand that shot a laser of digital numbers on the ceiling, revealing the time for a
man who must surely suffer exhaustion after returning
home from a business trip on the other side of the
world, one who would awaken confused and disori-
ented after traveling through so many different time
zones. The coffee bar she'd created within the alcove
that opened to the master bath, knowing how much he
enjoyed—and needed—that first kick of caffeine in the
morning.

   As she stared through a film of fresh tears at the
bedroom she'd designed with nothing but his needs
and preferences in mind, she vowed to do everything
within her power to create a home for him. She wanted
him to experience all the warmth and comfort that a
real home could provide, something she suspected
he'd never enjoyed as a child. The warmth and comfort that she suspected he still needed, even though he
was no longer a little boy…but a full-grown man.

   Yawning sleepily, Erik stepped off the elevator and
into his dark apartment. Anxious for the familiar comfort of his own bed after nearly two weeks of sleeping
in hotel rooms and airplanes, he started across the dark
living room. Halfway across the room, he stubbed his
toe on the leg of a ladder left in his path. Cursing his

secretary and her paint contractor for their carelessness, he gave the ladder a frustrated kick, then stepped around the obstacle, limping slightly as he continued on his way.

As he passed through the kitchen, he dropped his briefcase and garment bag on the floor, tugged his T-shirt from the waist of his jeans and kept moving as he stripped it over his head.

More asleep than awake, at the side of his bed, he toed off his boots, stripped off his jeans and briefs and crawled beneath the covers. On some distant level his mind registered that his bed was higher off the floor than he remembered, that the sheets he slipped between smelled fresher than usual and were much softer than he recalled.

The mouse's work? he wondered, then tossed an arm across his eyes, deciding he didn't care who had provided the soft, clean sheets. He just wanted to sleep and was sure that he could do so soundly for at least a week without ever once waking, given the chance.

# Six

Penny's mind awakened first, alerted by the unaccustomed warmth permeating her body. Wondering if the air conditioner had gone on the blink during the night, but too tired to get up and check the thermostat, she slipped a foot from beneath the pile of covers and tested the room's temperature with a bare toe. Finding the air cool, she drew her foot back beneath the covers and squinted a peek at the window opposite her. Greeted by a sky tinted the grayish-pink of dawn, she snuggled her cheek deeper into the down-filled pillow and closed her eyes. Just a few more minutes, she promised herself, then she would hit the ground running.

Though exhausted after working so late the night before, she still had a ton of work to finish before the weekend was over, which was why she'd opted to sleep at Erik's loft rather than drive back to her own

apartment, saving herself the time lost traveling back
and forth. Of course, since she hadn't planned to stay
overnight, she'd had nothing with her but her work
clothes and had been forced to sleep naked, something
she'd never done in her entire life.

Purring her contentment, she slipped one hand beneath her pillow and the other beneath her cheek and
nestled deeper into the soft down, deciding the warmth
provided by the mountain of covers created a perfect
cocoon for her body. Never having slept in the nude
before, she found the sensation of 350-thread cotton
sheets rubbing sensuously against her bare skin decid-
edly decadent.

As sleep washed over her again, drugging her
senses, she imagined Erik's surprise when he returned
Monday and discovered that she'd finished decorating
his apartment, just as he'd instructed. She was sure
that even as he'd issued the directive, he had doubted
her ability to complete the task within the allotted
time.

She just hoped he approved of all the choices she'd
made for him.

Two more days, she thought, yawning. Two more
days until he returned home. Two more days in which
to complete the transformation from cavernous, sterile
loft to warm and inviting home. But she could do it,
she assured herself, as she slipped closer and closer to
unconsciousness. Her incentive to do so had increased
a hundred-fold in the wee hours of the morning with
her decision to create for Erik the home he'd never
known as a child.

Sleep washed fully over her, and with it came a
dream. A pleasant and familiar dream. One that she
had consciously conjured hundreds of times over the

past ten years, though this one surfaced on its own, without any prodding from Penny and with a few slight variations.

In the dream she was with Erik, lying with him in his bed, his arm a treasured weight in the curve of her waist, his fingers shaped possessively over her breast. Her bottom was snugged closely to his groin, their bodies aligned as intimately as the bowls of the spoons she'd tucked into the cutlery drawer of the buffet she'd purchased for him from an antique shop on Sixth Street. Even as the silky threads of the dream spun around her, she could feel the warmth of his breath on her neck, the rhythmic rise and fall of his chest against the rounded curve of her spine.

She found both the dream and the sensations that flowed through her like warm, spun honey, more pleasant than usual. They took on a sensual quality, a heady eroticism that her dreams had never possessed before. Her subconscious reasoned that this was because now, unlike before, she knew what it felt like to be held by Erik, knew the strength and weight of his arms wound around her, had experienced the hardening of his body, had known the breathless expectation of what awaited her, them.

Need swelled, and she mewled softly, pushing her buttocks into the curve of his groin…and felt the lengthening of his arousal. She froze, her eyelids flipping up. With her heart pounding against her ribs, she blinked once at the bright sunlight flooding through the windows, telling herself that this was a dream, that it couldn't possibly be Erik pressed against her back.

Or could it?

Swallowing hard, she looked down at the arm snagged around her waist, then eased a hand from beneath her pillow and hazarded a touch. She jerked her hand back when her fingertips met warm skin.

But how? she asked herself, the panic rising. When? Erik wasn't supposed to return until Monday.

His arm tightened around her, and his fingertips squeezed at the fullness of her breast, making her gasp…and ache for more of his touch. She gulped, then swallowed, feeling his breath grow hotter on her neck, its rate faster. His fingers dug deeper into her breast and an arrow of desire shot to her belly, planting an echoing ache there.

She knew she should stop him. But how? And worse, did she really want to? Nervously, she wet her lips. "Erik?"

When he didn't respond, she eased to her back and found his head on her pillow, his hair mussed from sleep, his eyes closed.

"Erik," she whispered more insistently.

He moaned and snuggled closer. "Yeah, baby?"

Baby? He'd called her baby, she thought, melting at the endearment.

"Are you awake?"

Though his eyes remained closed, a slow grin curved one side of his mouth as he pushed his arousal more firmly against her hip. "Parts of me are."

Penny's breath shuddered out of her, while heat raced through her veins. She had to put a stop to this, she told herself. "Erik—"

He caught her hand, silencing her, then covered her mouth with his while guiding her arm around his neck. The need was instantaneous. Blinding.

And Penny tossed all plans of stopping him to the wind.

Tightening her arms around his neck, she drew him closer still, moaning as his taste surged through her.

An answering moan rose low in his throat, vibrating against her mouth. Growing bolder, she slipped her tongue between his lips, freeing the sound, absorbing it, allowing it to feed her desire for him.

Anxious to know more of him, she released her hold on him to explore the wide expanse of his shoulders, the padded muscles of his back. She thrilled at the taut skin that rippled beneath her palms, marveled at each corded muscle her fingers encountered. This is what she had waited for, dreamed of for so many years. This was the man who held the key to her heart, the man who had first introduced her to passion, the only man she had ever considered worthy of her virginity.

Though she had taken possession of the kiss, he quickly took it back, as if starving for her taste, for her. She relinquished control to him willingly, gratefully, wanting him more than she'd ever wanted anything in her life.

But even as her impatience for him grew, his lips softened, gentled, moving to press soft, tender kisses over her closed lids, her cheeks, her chin, then returned to her mouth and sipped lightly, deliciously at her lips as if she were filled with the sweetest of nectars.

He shifted as he took the kiss deep again, using the pressure of his mouth and the weight of his chest to press her back against the bed. She felt his hand light on her cheek, his touch as fleeting as the fragile wings of a butterfly fluttering against her skin, before his hand curved to cradle her jaw. He held her thus for a heart-spinning moment, his touch almost reverent. And even though her eyes remained closed, she was aware of the intensity of his gaze as he stared down at her, of the wonder that turned his eyes the deep, fathomless blue of the water they'd sailed over in Mission Bay.

Never had she felt more loved, more adored, more beautiful, than she did at that moment.

Then slowly he slid his hand downward, his fingertips gliding along the gentle arch of her throat, dipping into the shallow hollow at its base before finally settling over a breast. With his hand shaped around the soft mound, he slowly drew his fingers out, catching the nipple at its peak. He rolled the bud between his fingertips until it was nothing but an aching knot that mirrored perfectly her burgeoning need for him.

When she was sure she would die if he didn't take her, give her the satisfaction her body wept for, he released her to splay a wide hand over her abdomen. He dragged his fingertips down her middle, his touch only a whisper of movement, yet it left a trail of fire in its wake. His hand came to rest over the nest of her femininity, and the weight of his hand, the strength in the fingers that cupped her, was a pleasure so exquisite, so unexpected, tears burned behind her closed lids.

Blindly she reached for him, framed his cheeks between her hands and drew his head down to hers. "Love me," she whispered.

She didn't need to open her eyes to see his face and know his response to her request. His face, as well as his answer, had been etched into her mind and heart years before and spun into hundreds of dreams similar to this one.

Yet, as she traced her fingers across his forehead, along the high ridge of cheekbone, down the noble

slope of a well-shaped nose, she marveled anew at
each feature, the strength and handsomeness reflected
in each. She pressed her fingertips against his lips.
"And let me love you," she added softly and lifted
her head from the pillow to replace her fingers with
her lips.

She tasted the passion in him immediately, the need,
nearly wept with joy as he shifted his body more fully
over hers, his weight an indescribable pleasure she
knew she would never forget.

At his gentle urging, she spread her legs, making a
nest for him, then sighed her pleasure as he gave her
more of his weight. The gentleness he'd shown her
before was gone now, replaced by a hunger, a des-
peration for more. She felt the scrape of his fingers as
he slid a hand beneath her hips, lifting her, and she
arched instinctively to meet him. As she met his erection, she felt no fear, only a burning need to have him
inside her, filling her, ending this insatiable desire to
know him completely, to gift him with her innocence,
her love for him.

Holding her against him, he dropped his forehead
against hers, his breath a hot, desert wind on her face.
"This may hurt," he warned, even as he pressed
his sex to her honeyed opening. "But I promise not
for long."

She could feel the tension in his body and recognized it as his struggle for control, his hesitancy to
enter her as a fear of hurting her. Touched by his concern, his gentleness with her, she gulped back tears
and smoothed her hands over his back. "You won't
hurt me. You couldn't."

She felt the weight of his chest lift from her body
and opened her eyes to find him braced above her,

looking down at her. His eyes, filled with an unmistakable heat and dark with need, burned a path straight to her soul.

Emotion clotted her throat, and she was struck by a desire to give him more than just the home he'd never known. She wanted to give him all the warmth and love that he'd been denied throughout his life, as well.

"Let me love you," she whispered again, stroking her hands over his back and down to his buttocks. "Let me," she begged, and arched against him, taking him inside.

She watched the tension move across his face, felt the quiver of tensed muscle as he fought to maintain the control he clung to. And as he slowly pushed deeper and deeper inside her, she knew that he watched for any sign of pain or discomfort on her part...and knew, too, by the intensity of his expression, the caution in his movements, that at the first sign of either, he would stop.

She'd secretly loved him for ten years, but she was sure she could never love him more than she did at that moment.

When at last he reached the veil of her virginity and pushed through it, and she felt the painful tear of tissue never tested by man, she stiffened... But she didn't cry or beg him to stop. She wouldn't. Couldn't. Not when she had waited so many years to experience this, him.

*I'm going to remember this,* she promised herself as she swept her gaze over his face, memorizing each handsome feature, every nuance of emotion reflected there. *I'm going to remember this moment for as long as I live.*

And when the pain became unbearable, she closed

her eyes and dug her fingers into the cheeks of his buttocks, holding him against her...until the pain slowly gave way to pleasure.

As if sensing her body's acceptance of him, he began to move again, his hips a solid force of masculinity and strength against her softer, more feminine curves. With each thrust her pleasure increased, a web of vibrant color spinning crazily through her mind. Instinctively she began to move with him, slowly at first, wanting to capture each new sensation, each new wave of pleasure that rose within her. But soon the pace grew faster, the need for satisfaction a twisting pain, all but unbearable. She fisted her hands against his shoulders, pushing at him as she tried to escape both the torment and the pleasure.

But he wouldn't let her.

With her writhing and whimpering beneath him, he captured her hands and pinned them against the sheets at shoulder level. He held them there until she stilled, quieted.

"Look at me," he said, his voice sharp with a need as impatient as the one that held her in its grip.

Though she didn't want to open her eyes, something in his voice, in the increased pressure he placed on her hands, made her obey.

And when she opened her eyes and saw the passion, the heat reflected in his gaze...she knew that at last her dream had come true.

With her gaze riveted to his, her chest heaving beneath the weight of his body, she gulped back the emotion that crowded her throat and opened her hands beneath his.

He laced his fingers through hers and slowly dragged her hands above her head as he lowered his

chest to hers. ''Come with me,'' he urged, even as he
began to move his hips against hers again.

Every sensation and element she had dreamed about
through the years was there, a reality unlike anything
she'd ever hoped to experience in her life: the heat
that pulsed around her and slickened her skin with
perspiration; the need that paced like a wild animal
through her belly, searching for escape.

And Erik, the most real element of all: his breath
that all but seared her face each time he exhaled; the
blue eyes that held her captive; the long, strong fingers
threaded through hers that gripped so tightly, so desperately; the glorious weight of his body on hers; the
staff of throbbing flesh that joined them, making them
one.

Though a part of her mind wanted to stubbornly
cling to the notion that this was just another dream, a
product of her exhausted state, and she'd wake at any
moment as she had so many times in the past, she
couldn't deny that the need that burned through her
was real, nor could she stop her body from responding
naturally to the urging of his. She moved with him,
her hips rising and falling to meet each deep thrust,
her fingers vised around his and clinging, for fear
she'd fly apart if he released her.

When the pace reached a fever pitch, her thoughts
turned selfish, and she could think of nothing but the
need that rose like a mammoth tidal wave inside her,
the release that danced wickedly just out of reach. The
wave rose higher and higher, stealing her breath, her
ability to think, reason, then crested, tossing her high
on its peak. The wave curled and then crashed over
her with a suddenness that stole her breath and made
her body go rigid. She dug her nails into the back of

his hands and clung, as she was swept helplessly along, then dragged under. His name, a sound that seemed to form in her heart and swelled to push at her throat, slipped past her lips in a cry of sheer ecstasy as her body convulsed in a climax so explosive she wondered if she might die from it.

Then she was floating. Drifting along on a billowy cloud of the most exquisite pleasure, knowing that she'd glimpsed heaven. She wanted to pinch herself, scream her joy from the nearest mountaintop. She, Penny Rawley, who Suzy had claimed was very likely the last remaining virgin in their high school class, no longer held that distinction.

She would have laughed with delight over her accomplishment, but at that moment she felt Erik's body tense against hers, felt the painful squeeze of his fingers around her hands. She heard the low growl that built deep inside his chest, the shudders that shook his body...then the warmth of his seed as he emptied himself inside her.

Tears burned in her throat, stung her eyes as he sagged weakly against her and buried his face in the curve of her neck, his hands still linked with hers. She hadn't known, she thought wildly. She'd never understood that a man's climax drained him of his strength, leaving him totally exposed and powerless. But he'd known...and he'd trusted her enough to allow her to see him at his most vulnerable, to witness his weakness.

Tugging her hands free from his, she wrapped her arms around him. She held him to her heart, absorbing his warmth, needing his closeness, understanding as she never had before the emotional bond that sex forged between a man and a woman.

She was sure she would never experience anything again that would humble her more, yet produce, at the same time, such happiness, such a glorious sense of fulfillment, such a sense of completeness…until he cupped a palm at her cheek, turned his face to hers and pressed his lips against her throat.

Then she knew.

With tears flooding her eyes and her heart full of her love for him, she wrapped her arms more tightly around him and held him to her until his breathing slowed, until the perspiration began to cool on his skin. And when he slept, she released her hold on him only long enough to pull the comforter up over them both.

Pressing her lips against his temple, she whispered, "You're home, Erik. You're finally home."

When Penny awakened, sunshine flooded the bedroom and pushed stubbornly at her eyelids. She moaned and tried to roll away from the bright light…but discovered her legs were pinned.

Startled, she flipped open her eyes to find Erik lying opposite her, propped on an elbow, watching her.

Remembrance rushed through her. Kissing him, making love with him, holding him while he slept, their bodies still joined. She started to reach for him, wanting and needing to hold him as badly as she wanted to be held, but stopped when she saw the frown that creased his brow.

Unable to resist touching him, if only tentatively, she smoothed a finger across his forehead. "Is something wrong?" she asked uneasily.

He caught her hand and drew it to his lips. "No. I just thought for a minute—" He shook his head and chuckled self-consciously. "I know this is going to sound crazy, but while I was watching you sleep, I had this weird sense of déjà vu. As if I knew you. Before," he added, his frown returning.

Penny held her breath, sure that he had at last recognized her. And though she'd wanted him to remember her, prayed that he would and had been furious when he hadn't, she suddenly didn't want him to remember the shy, awkward girl she'd been ten years before.

As quickly as the frown had formed, though, it disappeared, and he was smiling again. "I guess I should say good-morning, huh?" he teased.

She went all but limp with relief. "Yes, I guess that would be appropriate."

His smile softened and he reached to tuck a lock of hair behind her ear, then brought his gaze back to hers as he drew his fingertips along her jaw to her chin.

His touch sent a shiver chasing down her spine and released a flood of memories of those clever hands touching her in other, more intimate places.

Without moving his gaze from hers, he laid his head down next to hers on the pillow and drew her hand to hold it against his chest. "I guess I should say thank you, too. That was quite a welcome home party you threw for me this morning."

*Welcome home party?* she thought in confusion, then stiffened when his meaning became clear. Surely he didn't think she'd *planned* what had happened? she asked herself, panicking.

He laughed softly and leaned to plant a quick kiss on her lips. "Not that I'm complaining, you understand."

Unsure how to explain to him that she hadn't plotted to seduce him, that she'd first thought his presence simply a figment of her dream, Penny could only stare.

He laughed and bumped a knuckle beneath her chin. "Talkative little critter in the morning, aren't you?"

She cleared her throat, knowing that she had to say *something*. But what? *Oh, I didn't really plan to seduce you. You see, when I realized you were in bed with me I assumed it was just a dream, the same as the thousands of others I've woven about you over the years.*

Hoping to avoid an explanation, she attempted to sit up. "Would you like some coffee?"

He hooked an arm around her waist and hauled her back down beside him. "What's the rush? It's Saturday...or at least I think it's Saturday."

"Yes, it's Saturday," she assured him, then tugged the sheet to her chin when she remembered she wore nothing beneath it. "I...I didn't expect you to return until Monday."

"Finished up early." He pushed himself up to an elbow again, never once moving his gaze from hers, as if he suddenly found her the most fascinating creature on earth. "I'd ask you what you were doing in my bed, but I'm afraid that might sound ungrateful."

She clutched the sheet closer to her chin. "I worked late and decided to spend the night. I wanted to get an early start this morning."

"An early start? On what?"

"Your apartment. The decorating," she clarified, when his frown deepened. "I wanted to finish everything before you returned on Monday."

The creases on his forehead slowly smoothed. "Oh." He gave the room a cursory glance, before bringing his gaze back to hers. "Nice job," he said, then grinned. "Especially the new addition to my bed." He shifted closer, placing his groin snugly against her hip and leaned to sip at her lower lip. "Though I'll probably have a coronary when I hear how much its going to cost me."

She braced a hand against his chest and pushed back in alarm. "I assure you that I kept my expenditures to a minimum. In fact, I did quite a bit of the work myself."

He choked on a laugh. "I wasn't talking about the cost of decorating the place. I was talking about *you.*"

Her eyes widened even more. "Oh, but I don't intend to charge you for the time I spent painting."

Laughing, he hooked an arm around her neck and drew her face to his. "You truly are naive," he said, before capturing her mouth in a deeper, much more intimate kiss. Just when she was beginning to melt, to have visions of a repeat performance of their earlier lovemaking, he bumped his nose playfully against hers. "Do your talents include cooking?" he asked, as he sat up.

It took Penny a moment to mentally catch up. "Well...yes. Though I doubt there's much in the refrigerator to make a decent meal."

He swung his legs over the side of the bed and stood, locking his hands high above his head and stretching them toward the ceiling. At the sight of his nude body, at the muscles that swelled and lengthened on his back and legs, Penny's mouth went dry as dust.

With a growl, he dropped his arms and leaned across the bed to give her a get-moving slap on the rump, then straightened and headed for the bathroom. "See what you can find," he called over his shoulder. "I'm starving."

Penny stared after him, her fascination with his near-perfect physique and his lack of modesty preventing her from immediately registering the directive he'd left her with. But as she slowly realized what he'd said, what he'd done, she shoved back the covers and pushed from the bed, blinded by tears.

She'd thought lovers awakened to cuddling, playful kisses and whispered endearments. And what had she received instead? Humiliation. A return to serfdom.

Furious, she dashed a hand over her eyes and grabbed her clothes. "The jerk," she muttered as she tugged on her jeans. *Him,* with his take-it-for-granted attitude that she would cook his breakfast for him. *Him,* with his less-than-romantic slap on the rear. *Him,* with his earlier inference that she expected payment for the "welcome home party" she had thrown for him.

The more she thought about his attitude as she stalked from his bedroom, the madder she became. She wouldn't be treated like some call girl summoned for a night's entertainment, she told herself as she slammed around the kitchen in search of something to prepare for his breakfast. It wasn't as if she'd planned to be in his bed when he arrived home. And she certainly wouldn't make the mistake of letting him find her there again!

She pulled the griddle from beneath the range and slapped it down over a burner. Then, realizing what she was doing, she snatched it right back up. And she sure as heck wasn't cooking his darn—

She shrieked, dropping the griddle, as strong arms circled her waist from behind.

"What are you doing?" she cried, trying to wriggle

free from the damp body currently wrapping itself around hers.

He nudged a wet nose against her ear. "I was lonely in the shower."

*Lonely? Lonely!* Seething, she closed her hands around the arms that vised her waist and tried to force them apart. "Then perhaps you should consider buying yourself a rubber ducky."

He dragged a hand up her middle and closed it over a breast, squeezing as he nuzzled her neck. "I'd rather play with you."

Penny closed her eyes, melting as he nibbled a path up her throat to catch her earlobe between his teeth. Feeling herself weakening, she stiffened her spine. "Tough," she said through clenched teeth. "I'm not for sale."

Frowning, he drew back and slowly turned her in his arms. When she refused to look at him, he crooked a finger beneath her chin and forced her face up to his. He raised a brow when their gazes met. "Whoa. You're mad."

She shoved at his hand and looked away, narrowing her eyes against the tears that threatened. "Brilliant deduction, Einstein."

"Was it something I said? Something I did?"

"Right on both counts." She jerked free from him, snatched her purse from the bar and stalked for the door, shoving the strap up over her shoulder. "I'm going home. And by the way," she called back to him, "my services are not for sale. *Not* to keep you company in the shower, and most assuredly *not* to entertain you in your bed."

Erik stared after her, dumbfounded. Her services weren't for sale? What the hell did she mean by that?

"Now wait just a damn minute," he said, charging after her. "I never tried to buy your services."

She stopped in front of the elevator and whirled. "You most certainly did. When we were in your bed, you—"

He leveled a finger at her nose. "That's exactly right. *My* bed. *Mine*. And I didn't sweet-talk you into it, and I didn't invite you there, either. I *found* you there. Remember? And if you're thinking about screaming sexual harassment, you can forget it, because I didn't force myself on you. As I recall, *you* came on to me."

"I didn't realize what I was doing. I was asleep." As soon as the words were out of her mouth, she wished them back, knowing how bizarre that sounded.

"Asleep!" he roared. "You expect me to believe that you slept through the whole thing? That you were never *once,* throughout all that heavy breathing and groping, throughout a climax that was probably recorded on every piece of seismographic equipment between here and California, you were never *once* cognizant of your actions or mine?"

She ducked her head and toyed with the clasp on her purse. "Not at first."

He tossed up his hands and spun away. "I don't believe this."

She snapped up her head, angry because he refused to accept her explanation. "You can believe whatever you choose, but it's the truth. When I first discovered you in bed with me I thought it was a dream."

He turned to face her again. "Dream?" he repeated slowly, then shouted, *"Dream!"*

She flinched and backed away. "Y-yes. A dream."

Erik stared at her, not wanting to believe her, know-

ing it was insane to think that *anyone* could sleep
through a lovemaking session the likes of the one they
had shared that morning and believe it was all a dream.
But he had to remember that this was the mouse he
was dealing with. The mouse who, while on their trip
to California, had metamorphosed in a single afternoon from a frumpy, scared-of-her-shadow secretary
into a gorgeous, if irritating, sex goddess.

And as badly as he wanted to discover differently,
he could find nothing but honesty reflected in the
green eyes that met his.

The mouse, he told himself again, his mind spinning
crazily as he remembered awakening to find her bottom nudging seductively against his groin.

Slapping a hand across the rods of tension on the
back of his neck, he turned away. "If that's what
you're capable of asleep, I'd hate to think what kind
of seduction you could pull off when you're fully
awake."

Penny's eyes widened. "Are you saying that I
was...good?"

"Good?" He turned to stare at her in disbelief.
"You were better than good. You were off-the-charts
fantastic. Fifty on a scale of 1 to 10. A man's ultimate
fantasy."

"Really?"

"Yeah," he replied, eyeing her warily as she took
a cautious step toward him. "Really." With her gaze
riveted on his, he slowly became aware of the amaze-
ment reflected in her eyes, the layers of doubt behind
it...and remembered that, for all practical purposes, he
was dealing with a virgin.

A virgin, for cripe's sake! No wonder she was act-
ing so weird. It was her first time, and he hadn't given

a thought to what feelings and emotions she might be experiencing.

*Or* what pain, he remembered belatedly…and a little guiltily.

"You're okay, aren't you? I mean…well…I didn't hurt you or anything, did I?"

When her face crumpled and her eyes filled with tears, he swore under his breath. Not knowing what else to do, he caught her hand and hauled her against his chest. "Now don't start crying," he ordered gruffly, patting awkwardly at her back. "I didn't mean to upset you."

She shook her head, smearing tears across his chest. "You didn't upset me. It's just that…"

When she hesitated, he pushed her to arm's length, concerned that he might have hurt her, after all. "What?"

She kept her gaze on his chest, dragging a fingertip around a circle of moisture she'd left there, while tears continued to stream down her face. "I'm not crying because I'm hurt or sad. I'm crying because you…touched my heart."

Touched her heart? Erik swallowed hard. He'd been accused of a lot of things over the years, but never once of touching a woman's heart.

And exactly what had he done or said that had touched her heart? he wondered, then made himself focus on what she was saying.

"You were so gentle with me, so tender." She sniffed and dragged her wrist beneath her nose. "Or at least you were when we were…" She dropped her gaze, blushing. "Well, you know."

Gentle? Tender? *Him?* Unsure how to respond, he pulled her back against his chest and tucked her head beneath his chin. With his arms wrapped around her, he rocked her slowly back and forth, trying to remember exactly what he'd done that she might have interpreted as gentle or tender.

He wasn't sure how long he held her before he became aware of her hands on his back and the tiny circles she was drawing on his bare skin with the tips of her nails. And once he noticed that, he couldn't help but remember the feel of those fingers vised around his, while they were making love. The way her nails had bitten deeply into his flesh, the way she'd clung to him, how she'd cried out his name when she'd climaxed.

And the entire time she'd thought she was asleep.

Which didn't say much for his sexual prowess, a fact that, now that he thought about it, shrank his male ego to the size of a small pea.

"You sure you don't remember anything?"

She withdrew slightly to peer up at him, her eyes moist, green pools of innocence. "Oh, I remember everything. It was just at the beginning that I thought it all was a dream."

Her response did nothing to soothe his ego but did succeed in deepening his frown. "At what point did you realize it wasn't a dream?"

Heat stained her cheeks and she dropped her gaze. "When...when my bottom bumped against your... well, you know."

Yeah. He remembered that part, too...as well as every detail that followed it. And damn if he didn't want a repeat performance, another chance to prove to her what a stellar lover he was...and another chance to judge *her* skills.

He crooked a knuckle beneath her chin and tipped

her face up to his. "How 'bout we give it another try?"

The color slowly drained from her face. "You mean…"

"Yeah," he said, and stooped to hook an arm beneath her knees. He hefted her up against his chest. "Only *this* time," he warned, as he headed for the bedroom, "I'm going to make damn sure you know you're not dreaming. You're going to remember every detail from beginning to end."

# Seven

Later that afternoon, while rolling a second coat of sage-green over the final wall in the loft's living room, Penny reflected back over the morning's events.

It shamed her a little that she'd allowed Erik to carry her back to bed without putting up much of a fight. Especially after promising herself that she would never let him find her in his bed again.

But she consoled herself by recalling her conversation with Mrs. Hilloughby and the glimpse of Erik's past his former secretary had shared with her.

*Children need their families, the assurance of their love, in order to learn how to give it themselves.*

He simply didn't know how to behave any differently. But he would learn, she promised herself. And by her example. And if his expressions of love were anything like those he revealed in bed...

She shivered deliciously, remembering the hours

they'd spent in his bed and the shower they'd shared afterward. She knew she would never bathe again without thinking of his soapy hands skimming over her body or how the water had pelted her skin, adding a new sensation to those she'd already secreted away, when he'd lifted her, wrapped her legs around his waist and taken her again.

Hunger was what had finally driven them from the shower, and the lack of food in his pantry was what had forced them out of the apartment and into making a trip to the grocery store.

She choked a laugh, remembering their shopping excursion. What a fiasco *that* had been. Her six-year-old niece, Rachel, possessed a better sense of nutrition than Erik. He had charged down the aisles, filling their grocery cart with every piece of junk food they passed. She had run herself ragged, trying to keep up with him, while returning the unwanted items to the shelves and slipping more nutritious foods into their cart.

"Where'd you put the Ding-Dongs?"

Penny tensed at Erik's shouted request, then forced herself to relax and place the roller against the wall. "On the grocery shelf where they belong."

"You put 'em back?"

She turned to find him standing in the doorway, his hands braced low on his hips. "Yes," she replied patiently. "Eat a banana instead."

"I don't want a banana. I want a Ding-Dong."

His stubborn expression looked so much like that of a pouty-faced two-year-old, she couldn't help but laugh.

He stepped into the room, his scowl deepening. "What's so funny?"

Once she started laughing, she couldn't seem to

stop. She held her stomach with one hand while weakly waving the paint roller at him with the other. "You," she finally managed to say.

He took another step toward her. "And what did I do that was so funny?"

"You didn't *do* anything. It's your face."

He dragged the back of his hand across his mouth as if she'd suggested he had something on it. "What's wrong with my face?"

She shook her head and dropped the paint roller into the tray, her laughter slowly fading. Plucking a rag from one of the ladder's rungs, she wiped her hands. "Nothing…other than the fact that you look like a two-year-old all swelled up in a pout because he isn't getting his way."

"So I like Ding-Dongs. Big deal."

"See?" she said, pointing to the arms he'd folded stubbornly across his chest. "You're doing it again."

"Doing *what?*"

"That pouty thing." She tossed the rag aside and stooped to pick up the paint roller. "But believe me, you're wasting your time trying that particular tactic with me. I'm immune to temper tantrums. I witnessed enough with my nieces and nephew to learn that the best defense is to just ignore them."

"So you're planning to ignore me?"

She lifted the roller high and ran it down the wall. "Uh-huh."

"And you think that'll make me forget about the Ding-Dongs?"

"Uh-huh." She straightened, lifting the roller high for another swipe.

"Wrong, buffalo-breath."

She whirled, her mouth dropping open. "Buffalo-breath!"

He folded his arms across his chest, smirking. "Yeah. Buffalo-breath. That's what us two-year-olds do when pouting doesn't work. We stoop to name calling."

She pressed her lips together, turned her back on him and resumed her painting. "Sticks and stones may break my bones, but words shall never harm me."

"I'm rubber and you're glue, so whatever you say bounces off me and sticks to you."

She gave him a withering look over her shoulder. "How utterly childish."

"I *want* my Ding-Dongs."

She huffed a breath as she dragged the roller down the wall, trying her best to ignore him. "I told you I put them back on the shelf."

"I *want* my Ding-Dongs."

"Oh, for heaven's sake!" she cried, and turned to drop the roller back into the tray. "We don't have any Ding-Dongs. Now be a good boy and go eat a banana."

"I don't want a banana."

"Well, we don't have any Ding-Dongs, so you are just going to have to find something else to snack on."

He took a step toward her. "All right."

Penny eyed him suspiciously, not trusting his sudden capitulation. "All right, what?"

He grabbed her arm before she could dodge him and hauled her up against his chest. "All right," he said, and began to nibble his way up her neck. "I'll snack on something else."

She batted at his head, laughing. "Stop that! I'm not a snack."

"Mmm. I don't know." He nipped playfully at her earlobe. "You taste pretty good to me."

A shiver chased down her spine. "Don't," she ordered, feeling the heat spreading quickly to her limbs.

"Don't what?"

"Don't do that. You're distracting me, and I've got work to do."

"Work?" He bent at the waist, tucked his shoulder into her stomach, then straightened and flipped her over his shoulder. "Work can wait," he told her as he headed for the bedroom. "*This* can't."

Later that evening, Penny sat propped beside Erik in bed, wearing one of his T-shirts, while they watched a video movie. Their backs were supported by a cushiony mound of pillows, and a bowl of popcorn wobbled precariously on top of their entwined legs. On the bedside table, a half-empty bottle of wine continued to chill. She was surprised that she felt so at ease with him in such a short time.

"He did it."

She dismissed his theory with a wave of her hand. "Too obvious." She popped a kernel of popcorn into her mouth. "The sister is the murderer."

He turned to look at her as if she'd just accused the pope of infidelity. "The sister?" At her nod, he snorted a laugh and gestured at the screen with his wineglass. "The sister had no motive."

"Spoken like a true only child."

Her wry comment won a frown. "You don't have to have siblings to know a murderer when you see one."

"True. But you do in order to understand why her sister might want her dead."

He reared back to peer at her. "That sounds dangerously close to the voice of experience speaking."

"It is."

"You mean you've seriously considered murdering your brother?"

She puckered her mouth thoughtfully, then shook her head as she reached for the popcorn bowl and dragged it onto her lap. "No." She fished through the bowl for an unpopped kernel and bit back a smile. "Although I have seriously considered rearranging his face on several occasions."

Erik hooted a laugh. "I'd like to be a fly on the wall when you try that maneuver."

Penny popped the kernel into her mouth and slanted him a frown as she chewed. "Are you questioning my athletic prowess?"

He gave her leg a patronizing pat. "Hate to bust your bubble, sweetheart, but there's no way a little thing like you could overpower a man."

"Oh, really?"

He set his glass aside, then shifted the bowl of popcorn onto his lap and turned his attention back to the television screen. "Yeah, really."

In the blink of an eye, Erik found himself flat on his back on the floor and the popcorn bowl spinning crazily just out of reach. Dazed, he heaved himself up to his elbows and gave his head a shake, not sure what had happened.

Penny lay on her stomach, her chin propped on her hands and her feet kicked up behind her, smiling smugly at him over the side of the bed. "So a little thing like me couldn't overpower a man, huh?"

Frowning, Erik pushed himself to his feet. "You

blindsided me," he grumbled. "Caught me off guard. Wouldn't have been able to do that in a fair fight."

"Who said anything about fighting fair? You merely stated that I couldn't overpower a man." She sat up and dusted off her hands as she settled back against the pillows. "You're just miffed because I proved you wrong."

"Get up."

She looked up at him in surprise. "What?"

"Stand up and fight me fair and square."

She sputtered a laugh. "Really, Erik. Do you honestly believe that I am going to fight with you?"

"What's the matter?" he asked, goading her. "Afraid you'll lose?"

She arched a brow in warning. "Don't push your luck, buster. I was raised by an older brother and learned early on how to defend myself. Keep it up, and I might not go so easy on you the next time around."

He grabbed her hand and dragged her to her feet. Positioning his fists before his face, he shifted his weight from foot to foot while punching the air between them. "Go ahead," he dared her. "Take your best shot."

She folded her arms across her chest. "This is ridiculous. I am *not* going to hit you."

"What's the matter, mouse? Afraid you'll lose this time?"

She dropped her hands, fisting them at her sides, and he knew he'd hit a nerve. Going for broke, he gave her shoulder a shove, knocking her off balance. "Come on, mouse," he said, taunting her. "Take your best shot. Let's see how tough you really are."

Furious that he'd called her a mouse when she'd

struggled so hard to prove that she wasn't, Penny doubled up her fists and led with a right.

Unfortunately, Erik's counter move to block the punch was a little slow. Her fist connected hard just below his left eye, and he staggered back, stunned. His foot landed square in the middle of the empty popcorn bowl and stuck there. He stumbled back another step, trying to shake free of the container...but lost his balance and toppled over backward. On his way down his head struck the base of a chest of drawers, and he slammed his eyes shut, moaning, as pain shot up his skull.

When he opened his eyes, Penny was on her knees beside him, her face so close to his he couldn't bring her into focus. Tears streamed down her cheeks and fell to splat against his bare chest.

"I'm sorry," she sobbed over and over again. "I didn't want to hit you. Really I didn't. You made me."

He planted a weak hand against the middle of her chest and eased her back a little, giving himself the room he needed to sit up. "I'm okay," he muttered, then groaned when pain shot from the base of his skull again. Feeling a trickle of moisture at his hairline, he reached behind him and laid a hand against the spot. When he drew his hand back, blood covered his fingers.

Penny shrank away, her eyes wide and staring, a hand clamped over her mouth. "I made you bleed. Oh, my God! I made you bleed!"

Erik pushed a palm against the floor and levered himself to his feet. "You didn't make me bleed." He gestured to the dresser behind him. "I hit my head when I fell."

She rose shakily, her face as white as the popcorn

that littered the floor around their feet. "But it's my fault you fell. I knocked you down. If I hadn't, you wouldn't have hit your head."

Scowling, Erik snatched a pillow from the bed and jerked off the case. He pressed the cloth to the back of his head, trying to stanch the flow of blood. "You didn't knock me down. I tripped."

"But you wouldn't have tripped—"

"For God's sake, Penny! It wasn't your fault!" Moaning, he sank down on the side of the bed and held the cloth against the back of his head. "Just get me some ice, would you? And kill the guilt trip. You're making my head hurt worse."

She spun for the door. "Stay right there," she ordered as she ran for the kitchen. "I'll be right back."

More humiliated than hurt by Penny's blow, Erik fell back against the pillows, nursing his manly pride.

Penny raced back into the room, carrying a plastic sandwich bag filled with chipped ice. She crawled onto the bed, slipped a hand behind his head and lifted it from the pillow. Easing down, she guided his head to her lap. "Here," she murmured soothingly as she placed the pack of ice on the back of his head. "This will stop the bleeding and help keep down the swelling."

Relieved that she was no longer blubbering apologies for having decked him, Erik settled his cheek on her thigh, closing his eyes as she stroked her hand over his brow and down his cheek.

Finding her touch soothing and oddly comforting, he nestled his cheek higher against the juncture of her legs. "That feels good," he said with a sigh. He felt the tremble in her fingers and frowned, fearing she was tuning up again. "Don't cry anymore, okay? I'm not hurt, and even if I was, it would have been worth it."

Her hand stilled, and she sniffed back the telltale tears. "How so?"

He rolled his head to look at her over his shoulder. "'Cause I figure you feel guilty enough to go out and buy me some Ding-Dongs."

Huffing a breath, she gave his head a push from her lap.

"Hey!" he cried, laughing. "Watch it. I'm hurt, remember?"

Immediately contrite, she drew his head back to her lap, though the "sorry" she offered sounded more grudging than sincere.

Smiling smugly, he nestled his cheek comfortably at the juncture of her thighs again. After a moment she resumed her soothing stroking, apparently having forgiven him. He closed his eyes, enjoying the attention.

"Stay the night."

Her hand stilled midstroke. "What?"

He lifted his head to peer up at her. "Stay the night."

"But…but I don't have any pajamas."

He dropped his head back to her lap. "Didn't seem to bother you last night."

"I…I need my toothbrush. It's at my apartment. I cleaned my teeth with my finger this morning, but proper dental care requires a toothbrush."

He chuckled as he snuggled his cheek closer to her warmth and closed his eyes again. "That's okay, buffalo breath. I have an extra one you can use."

The overnight Erik suggested developed into an open-ended living arrangement that Penny found difficult to explain, even to her best friend, Suzy, who had demanded a return to their old habit of meeting for lunch on Fridays.

Penny was already seated at the trendy downtown restaurant when Suzy arrived late, as usual, and wearing leopard-print capri pants and a black halter top. If her choice of attire wasn't enough to draw every eye in the restaurant her way as she tottered to their table on four-inch platform sandals, the silver belly button ring in her naval and the red silk scarf with which she'd tied up her hair—currently a Marilyn Monroe shade of blond—certainly would have done the job.

Though Penny didn't share Suzy's penchant for bizarre clothing and, at times, even more bizarre behavior, Penny understood that her friend used them to disguise her insecurities. Fast friends since the first grade, they had always shared their deepest, darkest secrets...a part of their relationship that, at the moment, Penny wished didn't exist.

"So are you officially living together now?" Suzy asked.

Penny pushed her Cobb salad around her plate, avoiding Suzy's gaze. "Not exactly."

"Well, what *would* you call it, then? You've been staying with him for over two weeks. I know, because I've tried calling you both day and night and always get your machine."

"I still have my apartment," Penny hedged.

"A technicality," Suzy said, dismissing the explanation with a careless flap of her hand. "Does Jase know?"

"About what?"

Suzy dropped her fork. "What are we talking about

here? The Lakers' current rankings? We're talking about your living arrangements! Now, answer the question. Does Jase know?''

''He...well...no,'' Penny finally admitted, her cheeks flaming. ''I haven't told him yet.''

Suzy buried her face in her hands. ''Oh, Lord,'' she moaned. ''When he finds out, he's going to blame all this on me.''

Penny knew Suzy's prediction wasn't an exaggeration. Jase *would* blame her friend, just as he'd blamed Suzy for Penny's decision to leave the ranch. Just as he'd blamed Suzy for everything Penny had done since the first grade that he considered an act of rebellion. ''Don't worry,'' she assured her friend. ''I'll tell him you had nothing to do with it.''

Suzy dropped her hands to her lap, revealing a scowl. ''Yeah, like he'd even hear you. He's going to be hauling your fanny back to the ranch so fast he won't hear anything but screaming tires.''

Penny shuddered, knowing Suzy wasn't stretching the truth by much. If Jase were to discover where she was living and who she was living with, he *would* haul her back home...but not before extracting a piece of Erik's hide as punishment for stealing his sister's innocence and ruining her pristine reputation.

Wincing, she glanced up at Suzy. ''You won't tell him, will you?''

Suzy pressed the tip of one lime-green lacquered nail to her chest. ''Me?'' she asked, then snorted a bitter laugh. ''Yeah, right. Like I'd tell the bear *anything,* much less something that would jeopardize your happiness.'' Her expression melted to one of concern and she reached across the table to close a hand over Penny's. ''You *are* happy, aren't you?''

Penny laughed and squeezed her friend's hand. "Definitely. Erik's everything I've always dreamed of and more. He's handsome, intelligent and so much fun to be with."

Suzy refused to be convinced. "What about in bed? How does he rate there?"

"Suzy!"

"That bad, huh?"

"Bad!" Penny echoed, then clamped her lips together and glanced around at the other diners. After making certain that no one was listening to their conversation, she leaned across the table, but lowered her voice. "He's fantastic. Unbelievable. Every woman's erotic fantasy come to life." She sank back in her chair and fanned her face with her napkin. "Just thinking about him makes me...well, you know."

Anxious to hear the details, Suzy scooted her chair closer to the table. "That good, huh?"

"Better than anything even *you* can imagine. But it's so much more than just the sex," Penny added, her expression turning dreamy. "Erik is...he's..." Unable to think of a word that would adequately describe him, she sighed and said, "Perfect."

Suzy drew back in alarm. "You're not falling in love with this guy, are you?"

Penny sputtered a laugh. "I've *always* been in love with Erik. You know that."

"Yeah," Suzy said uneasily. "But that was just smoke. An illusion. A teenage dream you've clung to. But *this*," she said, gesturing wildly. "This sounds totally realistic. Fatal. And what about him? Does he feel the same way about you?"

Penny caught her lower lip between her teeth. "I'm not sure," she replied uncertainly, then, seeing the storm building in Suzy's eyes, quickly added, "I know he cares for me. He just isn't one to express his emotions. You see," she explained, hoping to smooth Suzy's ruffled feathers, "his parents had little to do with him while he was growing up, leaving his care up to their household staff. As a result he never learned how to properly convey his feelings."

Suzy tossed her hands up in the air. "Would you listen to yourself! You're making excuses for him."

"Oh, but I'm not!"

"Yes, you are. And if you're not careful, he's going to break your heart. I've been around enough men to know that when one avoids using the *L* word around a woman, especially a woman he's sleeping with, it usually means one of two things—he's either married and has a wife tucked away somewhere, or he has a problem with the big *C* word. Commitment," she added, to make certain Penny understood. "Which means he's just stringing her along, because she's an easy lay.

"Mark my word," she warned, wagging an inch-long lacquered nail at Penny's nose. "He's going to break your heart." Her expression grim, she sank back in her chair and folded her arms across her chest. "I'll lay money on it."

Haunted by Suzy's warnings, that evening Penny sat beside Erik on the sofa, worrying a thumbnail with her teeth as she studied his profile.

It was easy for her to rule out Suzy's first explanation for Erik's inability to tell her that he loved her. He wasn't hiding a wife somewhere. She knew that for a fact, because she'd followed his life through the news media too closely to have missed an item as newsworthy as his marriage.

But what about commitment? she asked herself. Had he avoided telling her he loved her because he feared making a commitment? Was he really just stringing her along because he considered her an easy lay?

Firming her lips, she dropped her hand to her lap and curled it into a fist. No, she told herself. That wasn't the reason, at all. No man could treat a woman with the gentleness and tenderness Erik had their first time together, and each time since, if he considered her nothing but a convenient source for uncomplicated sex.

And she wasn't making excuses for him, either, as Suzy had suggested. She simply understood Erik's past and was willing to give him the time and the space he needed to learn to express his emotions.

Feeling somewhat better, she smoothed a finger along the creases that fanned from the corner of his eye. "You need to have your vision checked."

Absorbed in the report he was reading, Erik snugged Penny closer to his side, frowning slightly. "No, I don't."

"Yes, you do. You're squinting."

"Small print."

"Bad vision."

He glanced her way. "Nope. Twenty-twenty. I can see you just fine."

Huffing a breath, she wriggled free of his embrace and stood. "Yes, but I'm a bit larger than the print on those pages,"

He tossed the papers aside. "Maybe a bit larger,"

he conceded, then waggled his brows, "but much more interesting."

She slanted him a disparaging look, then focused her attention on rearranging the long stalks of yellow gladiolas she'd placed in a slender vase earlier that day. "First thing Monday morning," she informed him, in a tone that brooked no argument, "I'm making you an appointment with an optometrist. And you're *keeping* the appointment, if I have to personally escort you there."

Erik didn't bother to respond, knowing a reply of any sort, whether affirmative or negative, would be a waste of his breath. In the short time he'd known her, he'd learned it was easier to go along with whatever Penny said than to dig in his heels and argue with her.

Though some might consider Penny bossy and her attentiveness smothering, Erik sort of liked the way she fussed over him and worried about him. Other than Mrs. H.—and a long-forgotten stream of nannies and housekeepers who had received payment for looking after him—no one had ever paid much attention to him or his needs.

Finding watching her restful, he locked his fingers behind his head. There was something comforting in her movements or, for that matter, simply being in the same room with her. What that something was, he wasn't sure, but whatever it was it filled him with a rare sense of contentment.

And though he knew his single friends would say it was the sex, he knew it was more than that, though he did enjoy making love with her and sleeping with her curled at his side. Just being with her was satisfying. Talking to her, teasing her, watching the way her eyes lit up when she was excited about something, and even something as simple as listening to her rhythmic breathing while she slept.

And he liked what she'd done with his loft, too, he reflected thoughtfully, glancing around the room. She'd created a warm and inviting environment that he looked forward to at the end of the day.

Maybe too much, he thought with a start, realizing that he hadn't made as many business trips in the past few weeks as he normally would have made. The change in routine alone should have set off an alarm or two in his head.

Frowning slightly, he shifted his gaze back to Penny. But was it the improvements to the loft or having her there with him that made staying at home more pleasurable? Probably both, he concluded, watching as she deftly nipped off a bruised bloom, then turned the vase, angling it to its best advantage.

"You're pretty good at that."

She glanced up. "Flower arranging?"

"Yeah. That and more."

Blushing, she headed for the kitchen. "Like what?"

"Like a lot of things," he called after her, then pushed to his feet and followed. He pulled out a stool at the center island and sat down while she disposed of the bruised blooms. "You can cook as well as any chef. Decorate like a professional. Can whip things into order around the office quicker than any drill sergeant. And," he added, snagging her by the arm as she passed by him on her way to the refrigerator. "You're a damn good lover."

Her eyes widened in surprise, and he laughed. "Don't give me that innocent who-me look," he scolded, as he tugged her to stand between his legs. "You know you're good."

She lowered her gaze, watching her finger's movement as she traced the Cyber Cowboy logo imprinted on his T-shirt with the tip of her nail. "You really think so?"

Smiling, he nuzzled his nose in the crook of her neck. "I *know* so." He nibbled his way up to her ear and whispered, "Let's go to bed."

She pushed back in his arms. "But it's not even 9:00!"

Grinning, he slipped a hand under her shirt and smoothed it up her belly. "I wasn't planning on us sleeping."

He found a nipple and tweaked it, and she arched against his hand, then melted against him with a shuddery sigh. "What a novel idea."

"Yeah. I thought so." He dropped a hand to her buttocks and wedged her more firmly into the vee of his legs, then groaned when her abdomen bumped against his maleness. Impatient for the taste of her, he covered her mouth with his and thrust his tongue inside. Her flavor shot through him, pumping need into his already heated bloodstream and stripping his mind of everything but her. Her taste. Her scent. The satiny and pebbled textures of her breast beneath his palm. The slow, sensuous rocking of her abdomen against his stiffening sex.

He'd never met a woman who could arouse him so quickly...or one who seemed so oblivious of her womanly wiles. The combination was deadly, irresistible...enchanting.

"Penny?"

Her fingertips danced up his spine. "Hmm?"

"I don't think we're going to make it to the bedroom."

Her fingers stilled between his shoulder blades. "We're not?"

"Uh-uh." He stretched a hand over his shoulder, grabbed a handful of fabric and tugged his T-shirt over his head. Tossing it aside, he reached for the top button of her blouse. "New rule," he said, firming his lips as he worked his way down the frustrating row of tiny buttons. "No more clothes."

She sputtered a laugh. "What?"

"Too much trouble. From now on, when we're home, we're naked." He released the last button and straightened, but froze when he saw her stricken expression. "What?"

She gulped, then swallowed. "You said…'when we're home.'"

He slipped the blouse over her shoulders and let it fall to the floor. "Yeah. And that's what I meant."

She swallowed again, her gaze never once veering from his. "Yes, but you said 'when *we're* home,' as if you considered that I lived here, too."

"Well, you do. Sorta," he added, suddenly uneasy with the direction of their conversation, as well as the hope and expectancy he saw in her eyes. "Look, if you're uncomfortable staying here—"

"Oh, no," she quickly assured him. "It's just that at lunch today, Suzy asked me if we were living together, and I…I didn't know how to respond. Since we've never discussed our current arrangement, I wasn't sure how best to explain it to her."

Erik knew he was standing on shaky ground. He'd never given any thought to why he'd asked her to stay with him that first night, or any of the nights that had followed. He supposed he'd considered their relationship was based on a mutual need for satisfaction, the way every physical relationship he'd had in the past had been, and her staying with him was simply a convenience.

But then he remembered he'd never invited a woman to stay the night with him before, as he had Penny.

And he'd *never* experienced anything like the gut-wrenching fear that currently held him in its grip, knowing that if he said the wrong thing, did the wrong thing, she might pack up her belongings and move back to her own apartment.

Before he could think of a way out of the predicament he'd created for himself, or dig the hole deeper, she pressed her hands against her flushed cheeks and shook her head.

"I'm sorry. Forget I mentioned it. I never should've brought the subject up."

Feeling both a flood of relief that she wasn't going to demand a response from him and a burning shame because he felt that relief, Erik caught her by the elbows and drew her to his chest. He tucked her head beneath his chin and wrapped his arms around her. "I like having you here with me," he said, knowing he spoke the truth.

She slipped her arms around his waist and hugged him tight. "And I like being here with you."

If there was a tremble in her voice, Erik chose to ignore it. Instead he leaned back and tipped her face up to his. "Now where were we? Oh, yeah," he said, and smiled as he lowered his head to brush his lips across hers. "We were working on getting naked."

# Eight

Erik opened his eyes, blinked once, then bolted from the bed and to his feet.

Awakened by his cursing, Penny sat up, clutching the sheet to her chest. "Erik?" she called, squinting against the darkness. "What's wrong?"

"I can't find my damn jeans."

He flipped on the bedside lamp, and she put up a hand to shade her eyes against the sudden light. "Why do you need your jeans?"

"The alarm on my laptop computer went off."

Before Penny could process that information, he had snatched a clean pair of jeans from the closet and was tugging them on. When he headed for the door, she scooted from the bed. "Where are you going?"

"Downstairs. I can track him better with the equipment in my office."

Fully awake now, Penny grabbed her robe and hurried after him, shrugging it on. "What will you do if you're able to locate him?"

Scowling, Erik stepped onto the elevator and whacked an angry fist against the Down button. "Kill the bastard," he muttered darkly.

Eyes wide, Penny quickly hopped onto the elevator behind him, staring at the back of his head in shocked silence until the doors opened on the executive floor.

Erik stormed out with Penny one step behind him. "Can I do anything to help?" she asked, having to run to keep up with his longer stride.

"Yeah. Stay out of my way."

Hurt by his curt refusal, but determined to remain close in case he seriously intended to commit murder, she pressed her lips together and watched silently as he sat down before one of the computer monitors that lined his credenza. His fingers flew over the keys as he typed in the codes he needed to follow the hacker's movements.

Penny watched, mesmerized, as row after row of codes and numbers rolled across the screen.

"Dammit!"

She leaped out of the way as Erik shot up from the chair, swearing and sending the chair hurtling backward.

"What's wrong?" she cried, frightened by the thunderous look on his face.

"He's here," he snapped as he stalked for the door. "In my own damn building and using one of my own damn computers."

"Here?" Penny repeated and turned to peer at the computer screen, finding it difficult to believe that anyone could break into a building with a security system that rivaled the one at Fort Knox. Then, hearing the elevator ding, she whirled and raced from the office in time to see the elevator doors close behind Erik.

Fearing for Erik's safety—as well as that of the mysterious hacker, Boy Wonder—she headed for the stairs and raced down them. At the second-floor landing, she stopped and pressed a hand against her heaving chest, trying to catch her breath, before carefully opening the door a slit. She peeked out but saw nothing out of place in the empty hallway. Keeping her movements quiet, she pulled the door wider, slipped out into the hall, then held the door, letting it close behind her with the slightest of clicks.

She waited, listening intently for any sound that might indicate Erik's location.

She didn't have to wait long.

A loud crash split the eerie silence, followed by a furious roar that made Penny's blood run cold. She raced down the hallway, her heart thundering in her chest, and ducked into a large room, sectioned off into a dozen small work stations. Erik held Boy Wonder pinned against the opposite wall.

"Let me go!" the hacker yelled belligerently, kicking wildly.

"Oh, I'll let you go, all right," Erik growled and shifted to shove his arm across the hacker's throat. "Just as soon as the cops get here."

The hacker instantly stilled. "Don't call the cops, man. I didn't do nothin' wrong. Swear to God. I was just playin' around on one of the computers."

Erik increased the pressure on the hacker's throat, making Boy Wonder gasp and his eye bug wide. "You don't consider breaking and entering *wrong?*"

"I didn't break in. Swear to God. I work here."

"That's a damn lie. I own the place, and I sure as hell would never hire a punk like you."

"You didn't," Boy Wonder managed to choke out, obviously finding it harder and harder to breathe, much less speak. "Janitor...service. Work...for 'em. Clean the building...at night."

Though she'd kept her presence unknown up until that moment, Penny stepped forward, fearing that if she didn't intervene, and quickly, Erik might seriously injure his captive. "What's the name of the cleaning service?"

Boy Wonder jerked his gaze to hers. "Jupiter. Jupiter Janitorial Service."

When he named the correct company, Penny moved closer, in order to get a better look at him. Though he used language more appropriate for an adult, she was startled to discover that he was probably not much older than her thirteen-year-old nephew. His hair was long and worn in dreadlocks. Though his scraggly appearance was anything but encouraging, Penny couldn't stop the sympathy that rose as she wondered what circumstances would force such a young boy to work nights for a janitorial service.

Realizing how dangerous it was for her to feel anything but suspicion for someone caught red-handed breaking the law, she firmed her lips, steeling her heart against the well of sympathy already rising. "Who's your immediate supervisor?"

"Harry Rieser."

Erik glanced over his shoulder and shot Penny a furious look. "Cut the interrogation and just call the police, would you? This guy's guilty as hell."

Penny ignored him. "What's the cleaning schedule for this building?"

"Monday through Friday," the boy croaked hoarsely. "In by midnight. Out by four."

Her frowned deepened, as did her doubts that the boy was lying. "Are there any special instructions or restrictions on this job?"

"Shred all papers…in waste baskets." He winced and gulped a breath. "Don't touch nothin' on any desks. Nobody, 'cept Harry, allowed…on executive floor. Use bleach in toilets. Inside and out."

Penny knew then that the boy was telling the truth about working for Jupiter, as she, personally, had issued the directive that the toilets be cleaned with bleach.

She stepped up beside Erik, though her gaze remained on the young boy. "There's no way he could know all that, if he didn't truly work for Jupiter."

Erik snorted a disgusted breath. "He left out the most important restriction on this job. *Don't* touch the equipment."

"I didn't hurt nuthin'!" the boy cried, then snapped his gaze to Penny, obviously sensing in her his only hope of escaping arrest. "You gotta believe me, lady. I didn't mean no harm. I was just messin' around."

"Then why were you crawling around in secure systems?" Erik demanded to know, and won a strangled cry from the hacker when he shoved his arm more forcefully against the boy's throat.

Wincing, Penny placed a hand on Erik's arm and squeezed. "Let him go. Please," she begged. "You're hurting him."

"No more than he deserves," Erik muttered, stubbornly refusing to release his hold on his captive.

"But he's just a boy," she cried, then turned to the youth, tears filling her eyes. "How old are you?"

"Eighteen."

"Old enough to be tried as an adult," Erik replied with a smug smile.

The boy's eyes sharpened with new fear.

"The truth," Penny insisted, her gaze never wavering from the youth's. "How old are you?"

He gulped—an act made more difficult by the arm Erik still held at his throat. "Fourteen next month."

"You're only thirteen?" Erik shouted. "Why aren't you home in bed?"

The boy's eyes grew hard as he met Erik's gaze. "'Cause I like to eat."

Penny's fingers convulsed on Erik's arm. "But…your parents," she said, suddenly feeling weak. "Don't they provide for you?"

"Don't have any," the boy muttered, avoiding her gaze.

The strength in Erik's arm melted away, as did his anger. "You don't have parents?"

"No."

Erik took a step back, his arm dropping limply to his side. "Where do you live?"

Frowning, the boy rubbed a hand at his throat. "The streets."

Penny gasped, unable to imagine a boy his age living on the streets alone. "But where do you sleep?"

He ducked his head and lifted a shoulder. "Everywhere. Library. City parks. Anywhere I can stretch out, though bus stations are best. They're open all night."

Noticing the leanness of the boy's body beneath the baggy T-shirt he wore, she asked uneasily, "When was the last time you ate?"

"Yesterday," he replied, then scowled. "Some

dude stole my wad. Payday's tomorrow, though," he was quick to add, and gave his baggy jeans a cocky hitch, "so I'll be flush again then."

Swallowing back the tears that choked her, Penny turned to Erik. "Turn out the lights and bring him upstairs. I'll make him something to eat."

"Now wait just a damn minute," Erik shouted as she headed for the door to the hallway. "I'm not taking in any strays."

Penny whirled, her eyes sparking with fury. "Fine. Then I'll take him back to my apartment with me."

Less than an hour later Erik stood with his back braced against his refrigerator and his arms folded across his chest, scowling as he watched Boy Wonder shovel food into his mouth faster than Penny could put it on his plate.

Though it had galled him to do so, Erik had done as Penny had instructed and brought the boy upstairs with him to his apartment. And how could he have done any differently? he asked himself. Not when Penny had threatened to take the boy home with her if he refused. He narrowed an eye at the kid. And no telling what a punk like Boy Wonder would do to a woman as innocent and defenseless as Penny once he got her alone.

"What's your name, kid?"

The boy dragged an arm across his mouth, wiping away a milk mustache. "Jared."

"Got a last name?"

"Smith."

Erik snorted in disbelief. "Surely you can do better than that."

Jared dropped his fork and glared at Erik. "You got a problem with my name?"

Erik lifted a shoulder as he pushed away from the refrigerator. "No. Not if it's your *real* name."

"It's real enough. I got the papers to prove it."

Penny gave Erik a warning look. "No one is questioning your word," she assured Jared. "Would you like another sandwich?"

"No, ma'am. I'm 'bout to bust a gut already."

"No room for even a slice of apricot pie?"

Jared grinned and rubbed his stomach. "Well, maybe just a little one."

The tender smile Penny gave the boy deepened Erik's frown, and he moved to stand on the opposite side of the island from the two. "You never did explain why you were crawling around in secure systems."

The boy hitched a shoulder. "Just a game. Wanted to see where all I could go. Who I could outsmart."

"You must know a lot about computers," Penny said as she placed a generous slice of pie on Jared's plate.

He shrugged again before digging into the dessert. "We had computers at school when I was a kid. My teacher let me stay after school and play on 'em."

"Did your teacher ever tell you it's illegal to hack your way into secure systems?"

At Erik's question, the boy stopped chewing long enough to return Erik's glare. "Wasn't hacking back then."

"Then how'd you learn how to do it?"

"Messin' around."

"And what did you—"

Penny leaned to pick up Jared's empty plate, placing herself between him and Erik, and gave Erik a quelling look. "I think that's enough questions for one night." She straightened and forced a smile for Jared's benefit. "I'll bet you're exhausted. I've made the bed up for you in the guest room."

After settling Jared for the night, Penny returned to the kitchen where Erik waited, sitting at the bar. "I'll just get my things," she told him as she passed by on her way to the master bedroom.

"Whoa, wait a minute," he said, catching her by the arm and turning her around to face him. "Where do you think you're going?"

A puzzled frown creased her brow. "To my apartment."

"Why?"

She tipped her head in the direction of the hallway that led to the guest bedroom. "I can't very well stay here," she whispered. "Not with Jared sleeping just down the hall."

"Why not?"

"Because he's young and impressionable. It just wouldn't be proper."

"Then he's outta here," Erik said, and stood, prepared to give the kid the boot. "I should never have let you talk me into bringing him up here in the first place."

Penny caught his arm, stopping him. "You can't just throw him out on the street!"

"Sure I can. That's where he came from, isn't it?"

Penny snatched her hand from his arm. "Really, Erik," she said, tucking her arms beneath her breasts. "You can't be that unfeeling. He's just a little boy."

"A little boy who broke the law," he reminded her.

"A little boy who has no one to guide him or take care of him. He needs—"

The phone rang, interrupting her, and she exchanged a puzzled look with Erik before he snatched the portable receiver from its base.

"Thompson," he said curtly.

Penny watched his face, noting the frown that plowed his forehead.

"E-mail me what you've got, and I'll get right on it."

He punched the disconnect button, then replaced the receiver and turned to Penny. "I've got to go down to the office."

Her eyes grew round. "Now? But it's three in the morning!"

His frown turned to a scowl. "Yeah, I know. Unfortunately there's a rumor of a new virus that's supposed to be released within the next forty-eight hours."

"But what about Jared? You can't just leave him alone here all by himself!"

His mind already focused on the problem that awaited him downstairs, Erik grabbed the pie plate and a fork and headed for the door. "Then you stay with him."

Penny stood in the doorway of Erik's office, a cup of coffee in her hands, watching quietly as sunlight slipped between the blind's narrow slats, and streaking his hair with ribbons of gold, before tumbling down to paint wider stripes across the carpet. The only sound in the room came from the computer terminals lined up along the credenza, a constant hum punctured by an occasional click of Erik's finger on the mouse or

the sporadic, machine-gun-like fire of his fingers on
the keyboard.

That he'd worked through the night was obvious in
the slumped shoulders, finger-combed hair that stood
in wild tufts on his head, the dark circles that shadowed bloodshot eyes.

Her heart breaking for him, she crossed to stand
beside him and leaned to place the steaming mug of
coffee near his hand.

"Made any progress?"

His gaze riveted on the monitor, he hooked a finger
in the mug's handle and muttered an unintelligible response as he lifted the mug to his lips. He took a
tentative sip, testing the coffee's temperature, then
gulped half of it down before setting the mug on the
credenza again.

Shaking her head, she cupped a hand at the back of
his neck. "You're exhausted," she said, kneading at
the tension.

Moaning, he dropped his chin to his chest.

"Why don't you stop for a while," she suggested
softly, "and try to get some sleep?"

He stiffened immediately and sat up straighter in his
chair. "Can't. Got to figure this thing out. If I don't,
it'll shut down systems and companies around the
world."

Though she hated to burden him with yet another
problem, Penny felt her particular concern couldn't
wait. "I need to talk to you."

"Can't it keep? I'm up to my eyeballs here."

"No, it can't wait. Jared needs to go to school."

He narrowed his gaze on a row of codes. "So take
him."

"I can't just *take* him. He has to register. And in

order to register, he's required to have a legal guardian, which, as you well know, he doesn't have.''

Slowly he turned his head to look up at her. ''Please tell me that you're not suggesting that *I* become the kid's guardian?''

She opened her hands in a helpless gesture. ''I'd volunteer for the duty, but I'm afraid the courts wouldn't look favorably on a single woman taking responsibility for a boy Jared's age. It would be much more appropriate and acceptable if you applied for guardianship.''

Erik fell back in his chair and thumped a fist against his forehead. ''But I'm already providing the kid a place to sleep and enough groceries to feed a small army. Why do I have to take on guardianship for him, too?''

''Because it's your moral duty as a human being to take care of those unable to care for themselves.''

Erik positioned his chair in front of the monitor again. ''Leaves me out, then. I've been told I'm inhuman often enough to free me of that particular obligation.''

Infuriated by his stubbornness, Penny grabbed the arm of his chair and spun it around, forcing him to face her. ''Though I've had occasion to question your humanness myself,'' she said furiously, ''I know that beneath that thick skin of yours lies the heart of a warm and caring man.''

As quickly as her anger had appeared, it drained from her. ''Oh, Erik,'' she cried softly, and sank down onto his lap. She wrapped an arm around his neck and pressed her cheek against his. ''He doesn't have anyone else. Please say you'll do it,'' she begged.

Though Erik feared it was a mistake he'd pay for a

hundred times over, he found it difficult to refuse Penny. Not when she was sitting on his lap. And certainly not when she lifted her head to peer at him, and he saw the hope that filled her eyes.

"Oh, all right," he grumbled. "But you'll have to handle all the paperwork. I've got work to do."

She squealed and threw her arms around his neck. "Thank you, thank you, thank you," she cried, punctuating each expression of gratitude with a kiss. "I'll go right now and—"

Erik caught her by the waist before she could fully rise. "Do that again."

"What?" she asked, sinking back down to his lap.

"Thank me. I don't believe I quite got the message the first time around."

Smiling, Penny leaned into him and pressed her lips against his. "Thank you," she whispered, then flicked her tongue at the bow of his upper lip. When his lips parted on a groan, she said thank you one last time before slipping her tongue inside.

"Man! Get a room or somethin'."

Penny tore her mouth from Erik's to find Jared standing in the office's open doorway, a look of disgust on his face. Mortified that he'd caught them kissing, she shot to her feet, frantically tugging her skirt back into place. "We were just...discussing your future," she finished lamely.

He rolled his eyes. "Yeah, right. Like your tongue wasn't halfway down his throat."

Penny's mouth dropped open—her shock due partly to Jared stating the truth so accurately, and partly because she was stunned to hear someone so young speak so crudely.

Clamping her lips together, she planted her hands

on her hips. "You listen to me, young man," she lectured sternly. "I will *not* have you speaking to me in that tone of voice, nor will I allow you to use such inappropriate language."

Erik arched a brow, surprised by the level of authority Penny exhibited.

Jared stuffed his hands in his baggy jeans and slouched, sulking. "I just said—"

"I know very well what you said. There's no need for you to repeat it." She gave the hem of her suit jacket a smart snap. "Now," she said, lifting her chin imperiously. "I'm leaving to run a few errands, and you are to stay here in the office with Erik until I return. Understand?"

"Now wait just a damn minute," Erik argued. "I have to break this virus code before I leave for Virginia this afternoon. I don't have time to baby-sit any kid."

"I ain't a kid," Jared shot back.

"You *aren't* a kid," Penny corrected automatically.

"See?" Jared said smugly, hooking a thumb in Penny's direction. "She agrees. I ain't a kid."

Fearing by the look on Erik's face, if she didn't leave quickly, he wouldn't allow her to leave at all, Penny hurried for the doorway. "I'll take care of my business as quickly as possible," she promised, then whispered to Jared as she rushed past him, "Please be good."

"Hey, I'm always good," he called after her.

"Penny!" Erik roared. "Get back in here!"

Penny punched the down button on the elevator, then held her breath until she'd stepped inside and the doors closed behind her, ensuring a clean getaway. As the car started its descent, she sagged weakly against the wall.

*Please don't let Erik kill him while I'm gone,* she prayed silently.

After only a couple of hours alone with Boy Wonder, Erik feared he was in danger of losing his last good nerve. The kid was driving him up the wall. Not that he was being noisy or disruptive. It was just that Erik didn't trust him. And though he kept his gaze on his computer screen and the virus codes he was studying, Erik monitored the kid's every move out of the corner of his eye. And when the boy stopped before a terminal at the end of the credenza, Erik growled, "Touch it and lose an arm."

Jared lifted his hands in surrender. "Take a chill pill, dude. I was just lookin'."

Erik hunched his shoulders to his ears, the tag *dude* producing in him the same reaction as hearing fingernails scrape down a chalkboard. "*Don't* call me *dude*," he grated out through clenched teeth. "And *don't* touch *anything* in this office. Understand?"

"Hey!" Jared cried, sounding insulted. "I ain't doing anything."

"You *aren't* doing anything," Erik snapped.

A smug smile spread across Jared's face. "See? We finally agree on something. I *ain't* doing anything."

Erik sucked in air through his teeth, counted to ten, then jerked his chair back in front of his monitor. "Just stay out of my hair. I've got work to do." He scanned through the information displayed on his screen, found the place where he'd last read and began scrolling through the report again, studying the virus's complicated codes.

"New virus, huh?"

Erik glanced over his shoulder and frowned when he saw the kid was standing directly behind him. "Why don't you go play in the street or something?"

Undeterred, Jared braced his hands on his knees and continued to read over Erik's shoulder. He let out a long whistle. "Whoa, dude. That's some badass bug."

Scowling, Erik slapped a hand against the side of the monitor, turning the screen out of Jared's view. "If you don't mind, this is highly classified information provided by the Feds and *not* for public dissemination."

Jared turned away, flapping a dismissing hand toward the screen. "Like, man, that's kindergarten stuff. Anybody with half a brain could smash that bug."

Erik's fingers closed into a choke hold on the mouse. The kid was bluffing, he told himself. He had to be. There was no way in hell he could know how to block this particular virus. Not by just glancing at the codes currently displayed on Erik's screen. Erik had a *whole* brain, had studied the program half the night and he had *yet* to figure out a way to disable the virus.

He forced his fingers to relax on the mouse. "Nice try, kid, but I'm not buying that load of bull. There's no way in hell you could fix this one."

"Wanna bet?" Jared moved to stand behind Erik again and leaned to point at the screen. "See there?" he said, indicating a row of codes. "There's your hole. Plug it and you squash the bug."

Stunned, Erik stared at the screen. *He's right,* he thought, unable to believe he'd missed it. *The kid's right.* The fix was right there before his eyes and had been all along. He sank back in his chair. "Well, I'll be a son of a bitch."

"Tell me something I *don't* know," Jared muttered dryly. He spied a pair of hand controllers in the brief-case propped beside the monitor. "Hey, cool, dude!" He pulled one out to admire it, then glanced at Erik. "Wanna go head-to-head in a game of Stargate?"

Erik eyed him suspiciously. "You have a computer game on you?"

Jared dragged up a chair beside Erik's and reached for the mouse, nudging Erik out of his way. "Nope." He shot Erik a grin. "But if you've got Internet service, I can pirate one."

Erik plucked the boy's hand from the mouse and shoved it out of his way. "That's illegal. Besides," he added grudgingly, already reaching for the disk. "I own a copy of the game."

Jared reared back in his chair and swung his legs up, propping his sneakers on the top of the credenza while Erik fed the game CD into the slot. "Yeah, I know. I've played it a couple of times." He shot Erik a grin as he handed him a controller. "Wanna go first?"

# Nine

Still unable to believe how quickly red tape disappeared when Erik Thompson's name was mentioned, Penny stepped off the elevator and headed straight for Erik's office, anxious tell him and Jared the good news. She pushed open the door, then stumbled back a step, shocked by the sight and sounds that greeted her.

Erik and Jared were both leaning back in chairs in front of the computer monitor, each balancing a nearly empty liter of soda on their stomach while jabbing a hand-held controller at the screen. The sounds of an intergalactic war blasted from speakers, rattled the windows and shook the walls, nearly deafening her. Candy wrappers littered the floor, and a large, greasy box of take-out pizza tottered precariously from the top of the monitor.

Penny took a faltering step into the room. "What in the world is going on in here!"

Two sets of shoes hit the floor, and two guilty males shot to their feet, whirling to face her.

Jared ducked his controller behind his back and pressed a thumb against the pause button, stripping the room of sound. "Uh-oh," he muttered under his breath. "Busted."

She folded her arms across her chest and eyed the two furiously. "Yes. Busted. Honestly," she fussed as she crossed the room, stooping to pick up one of the dropped bottles that was currently leaking soda into the carpet. "I can understand Jared taking advantage of my absence. He's only a child. But *you*," she said, straightening and aiming the nearly empty bottle at Erik's nose. "You are an adult and should know better than to fill your system with junk food. And look at this mess!" She slammed the bottle down on Erik's desk. "And the language I heard both of you using. You should be ashamed of yourselves."

Jared ducked his head. "Sorry."

"Me, too," Erik mumbled.

"Well, sorry isn't good enough." She planted her hands on her hips, much as she'd done earlier when she'd scolded Jared before leaving on her errands. "I will not put up with this kind of behavior. You'll clean up the mess you've made to my specifications and satisfaction or suffer the consequences."

"Yes, ma'am," they said obediently.

"And when you're finished, you are both to come directly upstairs. Understand?"

"Yes, ma'am," they said again.

With a last scathing look at the two, she turned and marched for the door.

Jared flinched as the door slammed behind her.

Erik let out a lusty sigh.

"Damn, but she's pretty when she's mad."

Jared slanted Erik a look. "Dude, what're you smo-kin'? Ain't nothin' pretty about a woman with her panties in a knot."

Chuckling, Erik slapped Jared on the back. "Just shows how much *you* know about women."

Jared huffed a breath. "I know enough to know we don't want on her bad side. Now get your head outta your pants and start thinkin' of a way for us to get back on her good side."

Realizing the boy had a point, Erik pursed his lips thoughtfully, then cut a sideways glance at Jared. "Flowers?"

"Flowers! Man, if you want outta the dog house, you gotta chunk out some change for your ol' lady. Jewelry," he said, and used the toe of his sneaker to scoop a candy wrapper from the floor. He flipped it up high in the air and nabbed it easily, one-handed. He shot Erik a cocky wink. "Diamonds. No woman can stay mad when her ol' man lays diamonds on her."

*home friday morning remember no clothes e*

Though written in sentence fragments and without the proper capitalizations, Penny didn't have a prob-lem deciphering Erik's latest e-mail. He was coming home Friday morning and wanted to remind her of the new rule: no clothes while they were at home.

She scrolled to the next message. Three more days, she thought with a shiver of excitement, and Erik would be home.

*forgot tell punk hand's off my computer games e*

Laughing softly at his last message, she closed her e-mail program and shut down her computer. With her work completed for the day, she reached for her purse and stood. Just as she did, the elevator dinged, signaling its arrival on the executive floor. She glanced up as the doors opened and her jaw dropped when she saw a red-faced Suzy standing inside the car, her hand fisted in the neck of Jared's T-shirt, all but dangling the boy off his feet.

Suzy gave Jared a shove, sending him stumbling ahead of her out of the car. "Call the cops," she ordered Penny, then turned to Jared and pointed to a chair. "Sit."

Jared dropped down onto the chair so fast, Penny barely had time to blink, much less wonder what the two were doing together.

She finally found her voice. "What on earth is going on?" she cried, rounding her desk.

Suzy leveled an accusing finger at Jared. "This pervert tried to pick me up in the lobby."

The blood drained from Penny's face as she turned to stare at Jared in horror.

He slumped lower in the chair, scowling. "So I read her signals wrong. I thought the babe was sellin'."

Moaning, Penny dropped her face onto her hands. "Oh, Jared. How could you?"

"And the worst part of it is," Suzy continued furiously, "he only offered me a twenty."

Penny dropped her hands to glare at Jared. "You apologize right this minute, young man."

"Apologize!" Suzy cried. "Like hell. That pervert's going to jail."

"He's not a pervert. He's..." Penny struggled to

think how best to describe Jared. "He's Jared Smith," she finally said, unable to think of a better description.

"I don't care *who* he is!" Suzy raged. "Nobody's going to proposition me with an offer of a measly twenty bucks and get by with it." She stabbed a finger at the phone. "Either you call the cops, or I will."

Jared pushed his hands against the chair's armrests and heaved himself to his feet. "Dude, I'm outta here. This chick's trippin'."

Suzy flattened a palm against his chest and shoved him back down. "You're not going anywhere, unless it's for a ride in a police cruiser."

"Suzy!" Penny cried in dismay. "Jared's not going to jail. He's staying right here with me."

Suzy slowly turned to look at Penny. "With you?"

"Yes," Penny replied, suddenly feeling as if she were going to cry. "I'm responsible for him until Erik's return. He's Erik's ward," she explained, sniffing.

"Erik's ward?" Suzy repeated, turning to stare at Jared.

"Yes. It was official yesterday when Erik signed the legal documents I overnighted to him."

Suzy blinked once, then stooped, pushing her face close to Jared's. Wrinkling her nose in distaste, she reached out and caught a dreadlock between thumb and finger. "I'll bet he's got head lice."

"Hey!" Jared ducked away from her hand. "Keep your paws to yourself."

Suzy humphed a breath and took a step back, folding her arms across her chest. "When your niece wanted dreadlocks," she said in aside to Penny, "you threatened to shave her head."

Penny sighed wearily at the reminder. "Yes, I know."

Jared shifted his gaze to Penny's, frowning. "You got a problem with dreadlocks?"

"Well...yes," she replied truthfully. "My experience with the hairstyle has taught me that it is a haven for vermin."

Scrunching his nose, Jared scratched uneasily at his head. "Vermin? Is that like bugs or somethin'?"

Suzy smiled smugly. "If you're worried about what might be nesting in that mop of yours, I could cut it for you."

"Like I'd let you anywhere near me with a pair of scissors! You'd probably whack off my ears."

"No, she wouldn't," Penny said, quick to defend her friend. "Suzy is an excellent hairstylist. She cuts and styles her own hair all the time."

Jared eyed Suzy's mass of wild blond hair, currently twisted away from her face in tiny rows held in place at her crown by a colorful assortment of butterfly-shaped clips. "Swear?"

Penny sagged, relieved that the drama was over...and thrilled that Jared seemed to be considering allowing Suzy to cut his hair. "Triple-dog swear," she assured him, quoting a pledge she'd heard her nephew use.

Erik dumped his garment bag and briefcase on the living room floor and shouted at the top of his lungs, "Pen-ny! I'm ho-ome!"

He heard her squeal of delight from the kitchen and ripped off his T-shirt, prepared to be stripped down to nothing by the time she rushed into the room to greet him wearing only a smile. He'd imagined this moment throughout his week-long meetings at FBI headquarters and throughout the flight home from Virginia. He'd even broken every speed limit posted between the airport and his apartment, he was so anxious to enact it.

Grinning like a loon, he toed off his boots and had his fingers on the snap of his jeans when she appeared in the doorway. His grin melted off his face. "You've got on clothes," he said, unable to mask his disappointment.

"Jeez," Jared complained, pushing his way past Penny and into the room. "Give the lady a break. She just crawled outta bed, and you're already wantin' her back in it."

If Penny's appearance had surprised Erik, the punk's threw his system into shock. "What are you doing here? You're supposed to be in school."

"School is starting an hour later today," Penny explained. "There's a teachers' meeting."

"Oh." Erik cut his gaze back to Jared. "What happened to you? Did you get your head caught in a fan?"

Sheepishly, Jared combed his fingers through his freshly shorn hair. "Suzy gave me a peel."

"Suzy?"

"Suzy," Penny repeated. "You know. The friend I have lunch with every Friday."

In spite of his efforts to do otherwise, Erik couldn't take his eyes off Jared. "Oh. That Suzy." He gave his head a shake, trying to absorb the dramatic change in the kid in just a week. "New clothes, too?"

Jared scuffed the toe of his new sneakers on the scored concrete floor. "Yeah. Penny thought I needed some new rags." He ducked his head and scuffed his toe again. "Like anybody's gonna notice what I wear."

"Oh, they'll notice all right," Penny assured him, fussing with the collar of his freshly ironed tropical-print shirt. "You're going to make all the girls swoon."

"Swoon?" Jared hooted a laugh, then shocked Erik even more by dropping a quick kiss on Penny's cheek. "Woman, this is the new millennium. It ain't the dark ages anymore."

"*Isn't* the dark ages," Penny corrected and locked her fingers together at her waist to keep from brushing a lock of hair from the boy's forehead.

Jared grinned and shot Erik a wink. "Yeah, that's what I said. It *ain't* the dark ages." He hooked a finger in the loop of a brand-spanking-new backpack and slung it over his shoulder. "Later, dude and dudette," he called as he headed for the elevator. "I got me a school bus to catch."

Erik stared until the elevator doors closed behind Jared, blocking his view of the boy, then shook his head again and turned to peer at Penny. "Was that the same kid I was playing Stargate with last week?"

Beaming, Penny crossed to loop her arm through his. "Yes, and isn't he just the most handsome young man you've ever seen?"

With Penny's breast pressed against his side, Erik forgot all about Jared and his new look and remembered why he'd been in such a rush to reach home. "Yeah. Handsome," he agreed and turned Penny into his arms. He smiled down at her. "But not as handsome as me."

She melted against him. "Maybe," she replied

coyly, then laughed at his wounded look and gave him a quick hug. "Did you have a good trip?"

Placated for the moment, he slid his hands to her buttocks. "Mission accomplished."

"I never expected any less." She slipped from his arms and caught his hand, tugging him toward the kitchen. "Have you had breakfast?"

"Yeah. On the plane. But I'm still hungry." He pulled her to a stop. "For you," he added, and scooped her off her feet and into his arms. He dipped his head over hers, captured her mouth with his and headed straight for the bedroom.

He didn't break the kiss until his knees bumped the side of the mattress. He dumped Penny unceremoniously onto the freshly made bed, then planted a knee in the comforter and lowered himself over her. "You weren't planning on going down to the office anytime soon, were you?"

"Well, yes, as a matter of fact, I—"

"Uh-uh," he informed her, and reached for the top button of her blouse. "You're not going anywhere. Not for a long, long time."

The heat in his eyes stole Penny's breath, but before she could draw another, he had ripped open her blouse and closed his mouth over a lace-covered breast. He drew her deeply inside, and she arched, gasping, then shuddered as he a dragged a hand up the inside of her thigh and slipped a finger inside her panties and stroked the length of her folds. Heat shot to her center and burned, and she fisted her shoulders against his shoulders.

It's too much, she thought wildly, too fast! She couldn't think. Couldn't breathe.

But before she could beg him to slow down, he slid

a finger inside her, and she knew it wasn't nearly enough. Impatient to have all of him, she grabbed for his zipper, ripped it down.

"Hurry. Please," she begged, pushing at the waist of his jeans.

He rolled to his back and dragged her over him, bracing his hands on her hips, while he kicked free of his jeans. "I've been thinking about this for hours," he said, breathlessly and pushed inside. Her walls clamped around him, and he jerked convulsively. "Days," he confessed, groaning, then pushed deeper.

With her hands braced on his chest, Penny let her head fall back and rode him. Faster and faster to meet each hard thrust. Her palms grew slick with his perspiration, her knees burned from chafing against the comforter, the air became too thick to breathe. Yet, still, she rode him, watching the passion build on his face, thrilling at the tension she felt gathering in his body...and experiencing a sense of power she'd never known.

And when he climaxed, he took her with him, shooting her high over the edge. She closed her eyes and flung her arms wide, letting the sensations carry her, then drifted slowly to his chest, resting her cheek over his heart.

Still breathing hard, he lifted his head to press a kiss on her hair, then dropped weakly back to the bed and closed his eyes. "I could sleep for a week."

She smiled smugly. "Did I wear you out?"

He chuckled, and the sound vibrated against her cheek. "That, too. But I didn't sleep much while I was gone. Missed having you curled up beside me."

Emotion clotted in Penny's throat at his confession.

It was the closest he'd ever come to exposing his feelings to her. "I missed you, too."

He dragged her up higher on his chest and nuzzled his nose in the curve of her neck. "In the future, where I go, you go."

Pleased that he wanted her with him, Penny tipped back her head and smoothed a lock of hair back from his forehead. "That's really sweet, but you know I can't."

He tucked his chin to frown at her. "Why not?"

She lifted a shoulder. "One of us has to be here with Jared."

He settled his head back on the pillow and reached down to cup a hand over a cheek of her butt. "I'll hire somebody to stay with him."

Penny tensed, unsure if he was serious or not. "You wouldn't really do that, would you?"

"Sure I would. There's bound to be somebody out there desperate enough for money who'd be willing to keep a juvenile delinquent." Squeezing her buttocks, he raised his hips to meet hers. "I'm not sleepy anymore. How about you?"

Numbed by his careless remarks about Jared's welfare, Penny braced a hand against his chest and pushed herself up to look down at him. "But you can't just leave him with anyone. He's your ward, your responsibility." Frustrated when he began to nibble at the breast she'd exposed, she pushed his head away and sat up. "Erik! Listen to me."

Frowning, he drew himself up to his elbows. "I heard what you said. But it's not like I'm going to lock him up in a closet. I said I'd hire someone to keep an eye on him, and I will."

"But he doesn't need a baby-sitter!" she cried. "He

needs stability. Guidance. The reassurance that someone *really* cares about him.''

Scowling, Erik sat up, draping his arms over his
drawn-up knees. ''That wasn't part of the deal.''

''What deal?''

He waved a hand in frustration. ''Those papers I
signed. I agreed to serve as the kid's guardian. Provide
a home for him. Which I'm doing,'' he reminded her
pointedly.

Penny stared at him, unable to believe that anyone
could be so cold, so unfeeling. ''Surely you must feel
something for him?''

''Why do I have to *feel* anything for the kid?'' he
asked angrily. ''Isn't it enough that I let him stay here
with me?''

A knot slowly twisted in Penny's stomach. ''And
what about me?'' she asked. ''Am I supposed to be
grateful that you allow me to stay here, as well? Is
that supposed to be enough for me, too?''

He stared at her a long moment, then glanced away,
a muscle ticking on his jaw.

She slowly gathered the panels of her blouse together, suddenly feeling exposed...betrayed. Used.
''It's not enough,'' she said, fighting back the tears
that threatened. She swung her legs over the side of
the bed and stood, fumbling with the buttons on her
blouse. ''Not for Jared, and certainly not enough for
me. We need more.'' She buttoned the last button and
looked at Erik. ''We need your heart.'' A tear slipped
over her lower lash, and she dashed a hand across her
cheek as she turned for the door.

''Where the hell do you think you're going?'' he
shouted. ''We've got work to do.''

She braced a hand against the doorjamb, stopping

her forward movement, but didn't look back. "Home," she whispered, then added in a stronger voice, "I'm taking the day off." Choked by tears, she dropped her hand and strode from the room.

Erik didn't get any work done that morning. He paced his apartment, instead, waiting for Penny to return, telling himself that she'd be back, that she just needed some time to cool off. Once she had, he knew she'd realize how ridiculous their argument was.

But when noon came and went without a sign of her, his confidence began to fade. By two he was sweating and convinced he had an ulcer. By three his concern over a possible ulcer had given way to a chilling fear that he was suffering a heart attack. By three-thirty he was in the master bathroom, digging through the medicine cabinet searching for the aspirin that he'd read somewhere would ward off a heart attack.

He heard the elevator ding and, sure that it was Penny returning, raced for the living room.

But it was Jared who stepped from the car. Not Penny.

Grinning, Jared dumped his backpack on the floor. "Hey, dude! Where's the dudette?"

Erik turned away and headed for the kitchen. "Gone."

Jared trailed him. "Gone? As in *gone,* or just out running errands?"

Erik dropped down on a bar stool, braced his forearms on the granite counter and stared at his fisted hands. "Gone, as in *gone.*"

"Whadja do to tick her off?"

Erik turned his head slowly to glare at the kid. "Who said I did anything to make her mad?"

Jared shrugged and headed for the refrigerator. "Nobody. But everything was cool when I left for school this morning." He nabbed a soda and twisted off the lid as he lifted the bottle to his lips. He gulped a long drink, then dragged the back of his hand across his mouth. "The way I see it," he said as he hopped up onto the stool next to Erik's, "you said or did something that ticked her off, so the chick splits." He lifted a shoulder again and raised the bottle for another drink. "Doesn't take a genius to figure that one out."

Erik wanted to deny Jared's theory, but couldn't. Not when the kid was right. But he wasn't solely responsible for Penny leaving. The kid had played a part in her departure, as well. Unknowingly, granted, but their argument had stemmed from a discussion of Erik's shortcomings as Jared's guardian.

"Have you tried calling her?"

Erik shook his head.

Jared bumped his elbow against his arm. "Well, what are you waiting for, dude? That phone ain't gonna dial itself."

With a resigned sigh, Erik plucked the portable phone from its base. He stared it a for a moment, then frowned.

"What?" Jared said in frustration.

"I don't know her number."

"Give me that." Jared snatched the phone from Erik's hand and punched in a few numbers. "I need the number for Penny Rawley," he said to the operator who answered.

He waited, taking another sip of his soda, then glanced at Erik. "You want me to dial it? Or will you pay for them to do it?"

Erik scowled. "I'll pay."

Obviously satisfied with his response, Jared grinned as he pressed the phone back to his ear. After another moment of silence, he punched the disconnect button. "She ain't home."

"She isn't home."

"That's what I said," Jared said irritably. "She *ain't* home."

Frustrated that Penny wasn't at home, Erik pushed from the stool, dragging a hand over his hair. "Maybe she's just gone out for a while. Probably shopping. Women do that when they're upset."

"Maybe," Jared replied doubtfully.

"Well, where else could she be?" Erik cried, whirling to face him.

Jared lifted a shoulder, then raised the bottle and drained it. "Don't know for sure. Could be with Suzy." He dragged the back of his hand across his mouth. "Or she might've gone to see her brother."

A frown pleated Erik's forehead. "Her brother? How do you know about her brother?"

"She told me."

"And you think she might have gone to see him?"

"Could've. I know she was missin' him and his kids pretty bad."

That Jared knew that Penny missed her family and Erik didn't shamed Erik a little. "She's probably with Suzy," he said, forcing a confidence he didn't feel into his voice. "You know how women are when they're upset. They like to get together and complain about what losers we guys are."

"You could call her and see."

"Call who?"

Jared handed him the phone. "Suzy."

Embarrassed that he hadn't thought of that option

first, Erik stared at the rows of numbers, trying to remember Suzy's last name.

"Well, what are you waiting for?" Jared cried impatiently.

"I don't know her last name."

Jared snatched the phone from his hand. "Jeez.
You're really pathetic, you know that?" The boy
quickly punched in a series of numbers, then shifted
the phone to his ear.

"Hey, babe," he said, grinning when Suzy answered the phone. "What's happenin'?"

He laughed and slumped lower on the stool. "It was
okay, I guess. School's school."

He laughed again and dragged a hand over the top
of his head. "Yeah, the chicks really dug my new 'do.
Had to fight 'em off with my backpack."

Scowling, Erik punched Jared in the arm, gesturing
for him to get to the purpose of the call.

Frowning, Jared shifted out of Erik's reach. "Listen,
babe, is the dudette there?" He cut a glance at Erik
as he listened to Suzy's reply. "Yeah, he's here." Silence again, then his frown deepened. "Yeah, sure. I'll
tell him." He dragged the phone from his ear and
punched the disconnect button.

"Well?" Erik asked impatiently. "What did she
say?"

"She told me to tell you to go straight to hell."

Erik's eyebrows shot up. "Penny said that?"

"No. Suzy. She wouldn't put Penny on the phone."

Furious, Erik spun away, then whirled right back.
"That's it. I'm going over there and hauling her butt
back here where she belongs."

With a whoop of excitement, Jared hopped down
from the stool. "You go, dude!"

Erik was halfway across the living room, when Jared passed him on his way to the elevator. He grabbed the boy by the arm, jerking him to a stop. "Where do you think you're going?"

Frowning, Jared shook free. "With you."

"Uh-uh," he replied and strode for the elevator. "I'm going alone."

Jared trailed him. "But your chances of gettin' her back will be better if I'm there with you. You know how the dudette is. All protective and motherly and stuff. I'll just turn on the pitiful-little-orphan look, and she'll be climbin' in the truck with us before you can say Backstreet Boys."

Tempted, Erik vacillated a moment, suspecting that what Jared said was true, then shook his head. "No. You're staying here."

Jared huffed a breath and folded his arms across his scrawny chest. "You don't even know where Suzy lives."

His finger poised before the down button, Erik cut a glance at the boy. "And you do?"

Smiling smugly, Jared dropped his arms to give his new baggy jeans a cocky hitch. "Yep. Me and Penny went to her place the other night after we went shopping. Cool pad."

Another part of Penny's life that the kid was familiar with and Erik wasn't, he thought miserably. He'd never even *met* Suzy, much less seen her house. "Okay," he said grudgingly. "You can tag along. But keep your mouth shut," he warned as he stepped inside the elevator. "I'll do all the talking."

# Ten

———

Jared reached for the radio's volume control and gave it another twist. "Dude, you need some subwoofers," he complained.

Erik punched the off button. "Would you cut it out? I can't even hear myself think."

Jared folded his arms across his chest and slumped against the passenger door. "Like thinkin's gonna help. What you need is action." He narrowed an eye at Erik. "Did you buy her diamonds while you were gone, like I told you?"

Erik refused to make eye contact.

Jared tossed up his hands. "Man! When are you gonna start listenin' to me? If you'd bought her diamonds like I told you, you wouldn't be crawlin' on your belly right now, tryin' to get your ol' lady back."

Erik gripped his hands tighter on the steering wheel. "I'm not crawling anywhere. Understand? Penny and

I had a misunderstanding, and I'm just trying to straighten it out.''

"Sure you are," Jared muttered, then lifted a hand and pointed. "It's that house. The yellow one."

Erik flipped on the directional signal, then swung his truck onto the narrow drive, coming to stop behind Penny's beige sedan. With his gaze on the front door, he switched off the ignition and sank back in his bucket seat. Dreading the confrontation and, worse, unsure what he was going to say to Penny, he took a deep breath and reached for the door handle. "Stay here," he said to Jared as he shouldered open the door.

Jared was on the ground before the words were out of Erik's mouth. "No way, dude," the boy said, already jogging for the house. "Without me there to feed you lines, you'll screw things up even more."

Suzy opened the door at Jared's knock, a surprised smile spreading across her face. "Hey, kid. What are you doing here?"

"Came to see Penny."

"She's in the—"

Suzy clamped her lips together as Erik stepped onto the porch. Holding the door, she caught Jared by the shoulder and dragged him inside, all the while keeping her eyes narrowed dangerously on Erik. "She's in the kitchen," she told Jared as he passed by her, then stepped into the opening he'd left, successfully blocking Erik's attempt to follow him.

Feeling like a leper, Erik stuffed his hands into his jeans pockets. "I want to talk to Penny."

"Tough. She doesn't want to talk to you."

"Suzy."

Erik glanced beyond Suzy to see Penny place a calming hand on her friend's shoulder.

"It's okay. I'll talk to him."

"But—"

"Why don't you make Jared a snack?" Penny suggested quietly as she moved to place herself between Suzy and Erik. "He says he's starving."

"Fine," Suzy muttered. "I'll feed the punk. But I'm just a holler away, if you need me," she added, and blistered Erik with one last damning look before turning away.

Hugging her arms beneath her breasts, Penny stepped out onto the porch. "You wanted to speak to me?"

Erik's stomach knotted when he got a good look at her face. She'd been crying. Buckets of tears, if her red and swollen eyes were any indication. And he was responsible for every single one of them. Shamed by that realization, he curled his fingers into fists inside his pockets. "Yeah. I do."

She dropped her arms to gesture at the steps. "We can talk in the garden."

He stepped aside, allowing her to lead the way, then followed her down the steps and along a brick path that led to a garden at the side of the house. Beneath an arbor draped with wisteria, she stopped and turned. "Would you like to sit down?" she asked, indicating a pair of Adirondack chairs.

"Yeah." After she was seated, he dropped down onto the edge of the chair next to hers. Unsure how to begin, he leaned forward, bracing his forearms on his knees, and squinted his eyes at the sunlit path they had followed. Though he silently prayed that Penny would bring up the topic first, after several moments of silence, he realized that if any discussion was going to take place, it would be up to him to initiate it.

Stalling, he bent to pluck a blade of grass from between the bricks laid beneath the arbor and began to shred it between his fingers. "I want you to come back to the apartment with me."

"I'm sorry, but I can't do that."

He angled his head to peer at her and was surprised to see her cheeks flushed with anger. "If you're still upset about what I said about Jared—"

"Upset?" she repeated, her nostrils flaring. "Upset is *much* too mild a word to describe how I feel right now."

He tossed down the blade of grass. "Look," he said, twisting around to face her. "I know you expected me to be like a father or something to the kid, but that wasn't part of the deal."

"Would you please quit referring to your agreement to act as Jared's guardian as a *deal?* He's a human being, a young boy. This is his *life* we're talking about, not some cold-blooded business arrangement you've made."

He shot to his feet, his anger flaring to match hers. "It *was* a deal. For me, anyway. I agreed to give him a place to stay, provide for his needs, but I never *once,*" he said, stabbing a finger at the ground for emphasis, "agreed to be that kid's daddy. And if that's what you expect me to be, then the deal's off."

She shot to her feet. "And what of Jared? What happens to him when you renege on your agreement?"

When he didn't reply, the blood drained slowly from her face. "You'd let him go back to live on the streets again?"

Uncomfortable with the way she was looking at him, he dropped his gaze, shifting his feet uneasily. "If that's where he chooses to go."

"And how many choices does he have, Erik? He's only thirteen. You were his one chance to escape that life."

He threw up a hand. "Now wait just a damn minute. You're not going to heap that guilt on me. I didn't put that kid on the streets. He chose that way of life for himself."

"No. He chose it over life in foster care."

The news hit Erik like a blow to the chest. "Foster care?"

"Yes, foster care. When his parents abandoned him, he knew that's where he'd end up. And he'd heard enough horror stories about foster homes to know he didn't want to take a chance on being placed in a bad one. To avoid it, he went to ground, hiding out, working nights to support himself, while dodging the child services workers who wanted to make him a ward of the state and place him in a home."

She swallowed hard and dropped her gaze to stare at the fingers she'd laced at her waist, fighting back tears. "So, yes," she said, then tossed back her hair to meet his gaze again. "Technically, I suppose you're right. Jared did choose life on the streets."

Hearing her finally agree with him on something, did nothing to ease the numbness her disclosure about Jared's past had left him with. And it did nothing to ease his fear that he was losing Penny. And that's why he'd made the trip across town. He wanted Penny with him. In his apartment. In his life. Hell, he just wanted things to be the way they were before Boy Wonder had entered their lives.

"Penny," he began, and took a step toward her, his hand raised to cup her cheek. But before he could place it there, she took a step back, avoiding his touch.

"I'll talk to the judge first thing Monday morning."

"The judge?"

She laced her fingers together again and twisted. "Yes. I'll petition the courts for permission to take your place as Jared's guardian. If my request is granted, he can live with me. In the meantime," she added before he could interrupt, "I'd appreciate it if you would allow him to stay at your apartment. You needn't concern yourself that he'll be a burden to you while he's there. I'll see to his needs. I'll take him home with me each afternoon after work, supervise his homework, feed him his dinner, then return him to your apartment in time for bed."

Erik felt as if he was falling in a fast dive, the edge of the cliff he'd been tottering on suddenly having given way beneath him. Desperate to save himself, to hold on to the last thread that connected him to Penny, he grabbed for the one bit of control that remained.

The control he had as her employer.

"And how do you plan to do all that and continue to work for me? Part of *our* deal was that your duties wouldn't be eight to five. Before you were even offered the job, you were told that you'd be expected to work long hours, sometimes even travel with me, and you said that wouldn't be a problem."

"Yes," she agreed readily. "But it seems the demands on my personal time will soon change. To resolve your concerns, first thing in the morning my resignation will be on your desk."

Stunned, he could only stare, as the ace he'd held, the one last bit of control he had held over her, was snatched from his hands. "But you can't just quit!"

"I can, and I have." She drew in a deep breath and

squared her shoulders, never once moving her gaze from his. "Look at me, Erik."

He tossed up his hands and turned away. "Hell, I am looking at you and have been for the past ten minutes!"

"No. Really look at me." She waited until he'd turned to face her again. "Do you remember the young college freshman who wrote your English papers for you? The girl who earned you the A's you couldn't have managed on your own?"

"What the hell does *she* have to do with anything?"

"She has everything to do with it." She bit her lips to still its trembling, then said quietly, "I was that young woman." His eyebrows shot up, but before he could say anything, offer any kind of excuse for not remembering her, she plunged on. "And your inability to remember me just proves to me what a selfish and unfeeling person you truly are."

"Now wait just a damn minute," he began.

"No," she said, and took a step back, drawing away from him. "I think I've waited long enough. As I said before, my resignation will be on your desk in the morning. You'll have two weeks in which to find my replacement."

"I knew you'd screw things up," Jared grumbled. "I should've stayed with you. Talked to her myself."

With his eyes narrowed on the road ahead, Erik curled his fingers tighter around the steering wheel. "Shut up."

Jared slumped lower in the bucket seat, sulking. "Shut up," he sassed, then said, "Well, maybe *you* oughta shut up. It's *your* stupid yappin' that keeps gettin' us in trouble."

Not needing the reminder, Erik set his jaw. "I said shut up."

Jared folded his arms stubbornly across his chest. "This ain't my fault. If you wanna be mad at somebody, look in the mirror. It's *you* who's to blame. Not me."

Anger boiled inside Erik, fed by his frustration at his inability to talk Penny into returning with him, and he lashed out at the only person within reach…Jared.

He slammed a fist against the steering wheel. "It *is* your fault!" he shouted. "Everything was just fine before you came along. If it wasn't for you, Penny would never have left me."

Erik couldn't sleep. Not when with every breath he drew, Penny surrounded him, filled him…haunted him. Her scent lingered on the pillow he'd buried his face in and wafted up from the covers he'd kicked to the floor for the same reason.

But what haunted him more was her startling revelation.

He'd known her, he thought again, and rolled to his back to stare at the shadowed ceiling. He'd thought there was something familiar about her. Several times over the past few weeks, he remembered experiencing a flash of recognition, just a brief peek at a distant memory. He'd even mentioned it to Penny, tried to ask her if they'd met before.

But each time she'd cut him off or changed the subject to avoid responding.

Why? he asked himself. Why hadn't she wanted to tell him of their past association? Why hadn't she told him from the beginning, who she was?

Why didn't *you* remember her? he asked himself.

*Your inability to remember me just proves to me
what a selfish and unfeeling person you truly are.*

Erik shifted uncomfortably, her words biting deep.
Did she really think that poorly of him? Was he really
as selfish and unfeeling as she had accused him of
being?

Not liking the answer that surfaced, he gave up on
getting any sleep and rolled from the bed to prowl his
apartment, hoping to escape the guilt, as well as the
haunting memories of her.

But he quickly discovered that didn't help.

She was everywhere. In each room he passed
through, there was something to remind him of her, of
her thoughtfulness and care. The calendar she'd posted
on the refrigerator, noting scheduled appointments for
both him and Jared. The vase on the coffee table in
the living room, brimming with the fresh flowers she
fussed with until they were arranged just so. The sofa
she'd selected especially for him, its extra-long length
allowing him to fully stretch out, something he'd enjoyed doing with her snuggled at his side. The custom
drapes she'd had made for the windows that could be
pulled back to reveal a breathtaking view of Austin's
skyline or drawn when he needed to isolate himself
from the never-ending demands of the world outside.

Even the photographs she'd had framed and had
scattered along the sofa table brought her to mind.
Somehow she'd known the importance of each one of
them to him. The picture of him standing on the side-
walk in front of his building, his hands braced on his
hips and his head tipped back, wearing a proud smile
as he watched the installer hang the sign for Cyber
Cowboy International on the front of the building he'd
purchased. The snapshot of him with Red and Mrs.

H., taken when Erik was fifteen, not much older than Jared, still wet behind the ears, but wearing a cocky smile as he stood between the two of them, his arms draped over their shoulders.

Penny knew him, he thought gulping back the emotion that rose to his throat. Better even than he knew himself. And she cared for him, he thought, bracing his hands on the table and letting his head drop between his arms. In spite of the fact that he hadn't remembered her, in spite of the fact that he was selfish and unfeeling, she had cared for him. She was warm and loving and generous…

And he loved her more than he'd ever loved anyone in his life.

He gulped as the realization hit him, like a fist to the heart. Slowly he lifted his head. Was he too late? he wondered, panic tightening his chest even as the question rose. Would she give him another chance to prove that he wasn't the selfish and unfeeling person she thought he was?

He slowly brought his gaze into focus and found himself staring at the picture of him with the Hilloughbys. Memories flooded his mind. The night Red came to his parents' home to arrest him when he'd caught Erik hacking his way into government computers. Red taking him home with him, instead of to jail, when he'd discovered Erik was home alone. The summers and the afternoons after school he'd spent hanging out at their house, the hours Red had spent teaching him that there were more productive ways to use his computer skills than illegal hacking.

His hand shaking, he picked up the picture, recognizing for the first time the similarities between Jared and himself. Though their lifestyles were worlds apart—even when Erik was Jared's age—their lives weren't all that different. Not at the age of thirteen. Like Jared, Erik hadn't had parents who cared for him, either, though his parents had provided for his physical needs. Left on their own, both he and Jared had entertained themselves by playing on computers, testing their skills and their courage by hacking their way into places where they didn't belong.

He liked the kid, he admitted silently as he replaced the picture. In spite of Penny's belief to the contrary, he truly liked the kid. Jared was intelligent, fun to be with…

And Erik had threatened to let him walk back out on the streets.

He dropped his hands to the table again and hung his head, groaning. He wouldn't have let the kid go, he told himself. It was just talk. Crazy talk. Stupid yapping, as Jared had so accurately dubbed Erik's tendency to spout off when angry.

He lifted his head to peer down the hall toward the guest room where Jared slept. Seemed Erik had two people to convince he wasn't the selfish and unfeeling person Penny believed him to be.

And there was no time like the present to start making amends.

He straightened and rounded the sofa, headed for Jared's room. At the door he paused, remembering that it was the middle of the night, then lifted his hand and knocked, telling himself that Jared wouldn't mind being awakened—especially when he discovered that Erik needed his help again. This time to persuade Penny to give him a second chance.

When he didn't hear an answer to his knock, he opened the door and stuck his head inside. "Jared?"

he called. When he still didn't receive a response, he crossed the room, glancing at the bed as he leaned to switch on the lamp.

His heart dropped to his feet, when he saw that the bed was empty. "Jared!" he shouted as he ran from the room. "Jared! Where are you?"

Though he knew in his gut that Jared was gone, he checked every room in the apartment, then tugged on clothes and went downstairs and searched the other floors, as well, before heading for the parking garage and his truck.

"You're going to wear a hole in the bottom of that cup."

Lost in thought, Penny jumped, then carefully set aside her spoon. "Sorry."

Frowning, Suzy set her own cup down on the table. "He's not worth all these tears. Trust me. No man is."

Penny sniffed, dabbing a napkin beneath her nose. "So you've said."

"Well, it's true," Suzy insisted, as she rose to bring the coffeepot to the table. "Didn't I tell you he would break your heart?" She slammed the coffeepot down on a trivet. "Didn't I warn you that this would happen?"

Penny sniffed again, but was unable to stem the flow of tears. "Yes. But you failed to tell me how to keep from falling in love with him."

Suzy dropped miserably down on her chair. "That's because I don't know. Nobody does. It's all part of some cosmic master plan to drive women crazy. Men," she muttered. "They're all jerks."

"Erik's not."

Suzy rolled her eyes.

"Well, he's not," Penny argued, swiping a hand across her cheek. "He's just…different."

"I'll say."

"You don't understand. Erik can't help the way he is. It was the way he was raised. But it's there. I know it is. No one who is as tender and caring a lover as he is could be totally without feeling." Moaning, she propped an elbow on the table and squeezed her fingers around her forehead. "If only I'd been more patient, given him more time. I know he'd have learned to express his feelings. To open up to me and others. He—"

A pounding on the back door had both women jumping, startled. They shared an uneasy look, then rose and tiptoed across the room. Suzy grabbed a butcher knife from the countertop, then held out an arm, forcing Penny to remain behind her. "Who's there?"

"Erik."

Suzy snapped her head around to frown at Penny. "It's *him*," she whispered angrily, then turned back to the door and shouted, "Go away, or I'll call the police."

"I'm not going anywhere. Not until I see Penny. It's about Jared."

Suzy snorted a laugh. "Yeah, like we're gonna fall for that line of bull. Hey!" she cried, stumbling to the side when Penny shoved her out of her way. "What are you doing? Don't let him—"

But Penny was already flinging open the door. When she saw Erik's haggard face, she grabbed his arm and tugged him inside. "What's happened? Where's Jared?"

Erik raked his fingers through already wild hair. "He's gone. When I went to—"

"Gone! Gone where?"

Suzy tossed the butcher knife onto the table, fearing she'd be tempted to use it. "Who could blame the kid? I'd run away, too, if I had to live with him," she said, with a jerk of her head in Erik's direction.

Penny pressed her fingertips against her temples. "Suzy, please. This isn't the time."

Ignoring Suzy, Erik kept his gaze on Penny. "I don't know where. I was hoping you could offer a suggestion. I've searched the apartment and the other floors of the building but didn't find a sign of him."

Penny wrung her hands. "He could be anywhere. He's lived on the streets. He'd know places to hide where no one could find him." Her eyes grew round and she grabbed Erik's arm. "The bus station! Remember? He said he would sometimes sleep in the bus station, because it was open all night."

Erik was already heading for the door.

"Wait!" Penny cried, rushing after him. "I'm going with you."

The drive to the bus station took less than ten minutes, but it was the longest ride in Penny's life. As they raced along the dark streets, she prayed that they'd find Jared curled up in one of the chairs, asleep.

But when they arrived at the station, the terminal was empty but for the night clerk behind the counter. When questioned, the clerk assured them that he hadn't seen anyone matching Jared's description.

Disheartened, she and Erik had climbed back into his truck and made the drive back to Suzy's in silence. He pulled his truck up behind her car in the drive-

way, but didn't turn off the ignition. "I'll go by the
police department. File a missing-person report."

Though she knew it was the next logical step, Penny
shook her head. "That might cause Jared more problems. If he's classified as a runaway…" She caught
her lower lip between her teeth, unable to voice what
harm being classified a runaway could do to her hopes
of having him declared her ward.

Erik set his jaw, understanding her fears. "This is
all my fault."

"No," Penny said, her voice quavering. "You
mustn't blame yourself. Jared made the choice to run
away, not you."

Erik whipped his head around. "Dammit! It *is* my
fault. I all but kicked him out the door. Blamed him
for you leaving. Told him if it wasn't for him, you'd
never have left in the first place. That you'd still be
with me."

"Oh, Erik. You didn't."

Unable to bear facing the disappointment, the horror
he saw reflected on her face, he turned to stare blindly
out the windshield. "I did. I put the full blame on
him." He gulped, forcing back the emotion that rose,
then set his jaw. "I know it wasn't his fault. But I
was mad. Hurt. Needed to place the fault for losing
you somewhere. Anywhere but on me. Jared was
handy."

He felt the warmth of her fingers on his arm, the
comfort offered in the soft squeeze she gave it…and
wanted more than anything to bury his face in her lap
and cry like a baby. Guilt—and maybe a bit of pride—
was all that kept him upright and his gaze riveted on
the windshield. "I screwed up," he said, then shook
his head sadly. "Jared said I would. But what he

didn't know was that I'd screwed up long before he ever came on the scene.''

Digging deep for the courage to say it all, he turned to look at Penny. ''You were right. I am selfish and unfeeling. Always have been. But I want you to know that I did remember you. Not fully. Not as well as you seem to remember me. But I would have these little flashes every once in a while, and I'd almost remember. Like the afternoon we were leaving for California, when I picked you up and set you inside my truck. I felt as if I'd done that before.''

Her throat tight with emotion, Penny nodded. ''You had.''

He frowned, trying to recall the event. ''It was raining,'' he said, his forehead smoothing as the scene slowly unfolded in his mind. ''I was supposed to meet you in front of the tower, so you could give me a paper you'd typed.''

She nodded, tears streaming down her cheeks. ''And you offered to give me a ride back to my car.''

He laughed, relieved that he'd finally remembered. ''You were wearing a dress and high heels, of all things. I was afraid you'd ruin your shoes.''

She dropped her gaze. ''I'd dressed up, hoping to impress you.''

The laughter dried up in his throat at the embarrassment he saw staining her cheeks. ''I'm sorry, Penny. I was young, stupid and so focused on getting out of college and making a name for myself, that I was blind to anyone's needs but my own.'' He shook his head and reached to close his hand over hers. ''Which in no way excuses me from not remembering a girl as beautiful and kind as you.''

She glanced up. ''You thought I was beautiful?''

"You *are* beautiful." He eased closer to the console, squeezing her hand. "I know it's asking a lot, but if you'd—"

He swore, startling Penny, and spun around, yanking his hand from hers as he shouldered open the door.

Penny stared after him as he dropped to the ground and raced around the hood of the truck. "What—"

Then she saw him. Jared. Strolling down the side of the driveway toward them, his hands shoved deep into the pockets of his baggy jeans as if he didn't have a care in the world. She grabbed for the door handle, remembering how roughly Erik had handled him when he'd discovered him hacking, and fearing what Erik would do to him now for running away. But she stopped, her fingers curled tightly around the handle, when Erik grabbed Jared and lifted him up, hugging him against his chest.

She caught only fragments of what he said. Sorry...not your fault...back home...

"He cares," she murmured, blinking back tears. "He really cares!"

Jumping down from the truck, she ran to throw her arms around them both. The three looped their arms around each other and spun in a circle, laughing.

"Would you mind keeping it down?" Suzy yelled from the back porch stoop. "I've got neighbors, you know."

Still laughing, Penny turned and called to Suzy, "It's Jared! He's back."

Suzy rolled her eyes and clomped down the steps to join them. "Like I didn't already know that. He showed up right after the two of you left, looking for a handout."

Grinning, Jared slung an arm around Suzy's shoulders. "I was hungry."

Though Suzy wore a scowl, Erik noticed that she didn't try to pull away from the boy. In fact, though the light was dim and he couldn't be sure, he thought he saw her slip her arm around the kid's waist.

"You're always hungry," Suzy grumbled.

Jared preened. "Gotta keep up my strength so I can keep all the babes like you happy."

She ducked from beneath his arm. "Then get back inside and finish the sandwich I made for you, before I dump it in the trash."

Jared hesitated, glancing at Erik and Penny. "I don't know," he said, uneasily. "Every time I leave these two alone, something bad happens."

Already on her way to the house, Suzy looked over her shoulder. When she saw that Penny and Erik were holding hands, she did a neat U-turn and grabbed Jared by the arm. "Trust me, kid. He doesn't need your help anymore."

Penny laughed as she watched Suzy drag Jared back to the house, with him digging in his feet and arguing with her every step of the way.

"At least he won't be far if I find I need him," Erik said.

Penny glanced up, her laughter fading as she met Erik's gaze. "I think he needs you more than you'll ever need him."

Erik shook his head as he turned her into arms. "No way," he said, locking his hands behind her waist. "The kid's grown on me. I thought I was going to have a heart attack when I discovered he wasn't in his bed."

A shiver chased down Penny's spine, remembering

her own fears when she'd learned that Jared was missing. "I was pretty scared, myself."

"Penny…"

She swallowed hard. "Yes?"

He blew out a long breath, then shook his head. "I'm not any good at this."

"Good at what?"

"At saying what's on my mind."

Her lips trembled on a smile. "Oh, I'd say you are very good at saying what's on your mind."

"On my heart then."

Her pulse leaped. "Yes, you have seemed to have had a problem with that in the past."

He tightened his arms around her and drew her closer. "And I want to change that. But I might need some help."

"From Jared?"

He nodded. "Yes. Him. But you, too," he added.

This is it, Penny thought, her heart leaping to pound wildly against her chest. My date with destiny. She slicked her lips, suddenly uncertain of the outcome. "I've always found it was best to simply say what was in my heart."

"Really?"

She nodded. "It resolves a lot of uncertainty."

He stared at her a long moment, then swallowed hard. "Hold me," he said, his voice sounding rusty.

"But I am holding you."

"No. I mean *really* hold me. This is tough."

She wriggled closer, hugging her arms tight around him. "Better?"

He closed his eyes on a sigh. "Much."

When he opened them again, the uncertainty was

gone, replaced by a sureness, a warmth, that had tears flooding her eyes.

"I love you, Penny," he said quietly. "And I need you. More than I've ever needed anyone in my life."

"Oh, Erik," she whispered tearfully.

He lifted a hand and brushed back a lock of hair from her face, then cradled her cheek. "I want you with me, by my side, in my heart, sharing my life. Always and forever."

Tears slipped over her lower lashes and slid down her cheeks. He caught one on the tip of his finger and brought it to his lips. "We were meant to be together. It just took me a long time to realize it."

Sobbing, she threw her arms around his neck. "Oh, Erik. I've dreamed of this moment for years."

He frowned, then slowly drew back to look at her. "You have?"

She nodded, sweeping her hands beneath her eyes. "I've always loved you. Ever since the first time I saw you. For ten long years I've dreamed of you holding me like this, and making love with me. And when I saw your ad in the paper, I just knew it was destiny bringing us together again."

"Whoa," he said, holding up a hand. "Back up a minute. You dreamed of us making love?"

Suddenly embarrassed, she nodded her head.

"Was I any good?"

"Good!" she cried in dismay. "You were the best!"

He dropped back his head and laughed. "And how would you know, when you'd never slept with anyone before?"

Irritated that at a moment like this he would remind

her of her lack of experience with men, she pulled from his embrace. "I just did."

"Dude, I *knew* you'd screw things up again!"

They both turned to find Jared hanging out the living room window, listening to every word.

"Don't you know better than to question a woman's judgment?" the boy yelled. "Especially when you're about to pop the big question. Promise her diamonds," he shouted. "The bigger and flashier the better."

"Yeah," Suzy added, pushing her head through the opening, beside Jared. "And a car. A Porsche would be nice. A red one."

Penny planted her hands on her hips. "I'll have you know that I don't want diamonds and expensive cars. All I've ever wanted is—"

When she hesitated, Erik caught her arm and turned her back around to face him. "What do you want?"

"You," she said, tears filling her eyes again. "All I've ever wanted is you."

"Then I'll make you a deal," he offered, drawing her hips up snugly against his. "Promise me that you'll marry me, so that we can adopt that kid and teach him some manners, and I'm yours forever."

Her eyes widened, then, laughing, she threw her arms around his neck. "Deal."

\*     \*     \*     \*     \*

**SILHOUETTE® MAKES YOU A STAR!**

Look in the back pages of
all June Silhouette series books to find an
exciting new contest with fabulous prizes!
Available exclusively through Silhouette.

Don't miss it!

*Silhouette*®
Where love comes alive™

*P.S. Watch for details on how you can meet
your favorite Silhouette author.*

# THE FORTUNES OF TEXAS

invite you to meet

# THE LOST HEIRS

**Silhouette Desire's scintillating
new miniseries, featuring the beloved**

## FORTUNES OF TEXAS

**and six of your favorite authors.**

*A Most Desirable M.D.*–June 2001
by Anne Marie Winston (SD #1371)

*The Pregnant Heiress*–July 2001
by Eileen Wilks (SD #1378)

*Baby of Fortune*–August 2001
by Shirley Rogers (SD #1384)

*Fortune's Secret Daughter*–September 2001
by Barbara McCauley (SD #1390)

*Her Boss's Baby*–October 2001
by Cathleen Galitz (SD #1396)

*Did You Say Twins?!*–December 2001
by Maureen Child (SD #1408)

And be sure to watch for *Gifts of Fortune*,
Silhouette's exciting new single title,
on sale November 2001

*Don't miss these unforgettable romances...
available at your favorite retail outlet.*

*Silhouette* ®

*Where love comes alive* ™

Visit Silhouette at www.eHarlequin.com          SDFOT